FORESTS, FISHING & FORGERY

A CAMPER AND CRIMINALS COZY MYSTERY

TONYA KAPPES

GET FREE BOOKS

Join my newsletter.
and see all of my books on Amazon.
Find all these links on my website, Tonyakappes.com.

"You okay?" He turned around and asked when he noticed I wasn't walking as fast as he was.

"I've got to go potty." My brows frowned.

"One or two?" He held up his fingers.

"One!" I yelled, it echoed.

"Just go right there behind the tree. Not too far off the trail. And watch out for poison ivy. And hurry. We are almost done." He smiled. "Then we can go to your place."

"Just to check on Fifi," I joked.

"Yep." He snapped his fingers. "That's exactly what I was thinking."

"I bet you were," I teased and headed back into the wooded area, watching my step. I didn't want to step on any critters, like a snake.

"I'm lucky I didn't have sisters. My parents and I used to hike all of these trails." I could hear him opening up about his family. He rarely talked about his mom. "You would've loved my mom. She would've loved you. I mean, you're really girly but can hang with the guys when you want to."

The more he talked, the harder it was for me to concentrate on the task at hand. I started to get in position, with a tree trunk against my back to steady me. Peeing on myself didn't sound like a good thing.

"Come on, Mae," I encouraged myself out of this stage fright. "You've got. . ." I looked down at the toes of my boots. "What on earth?" I leaned a little more forward to try to get a better look. "Omg! Omg!" I jumped up and took off running while pulling my shorts back up. "Omg!" I continued to scream and dropped when I made it back to the trail.

"What is wrong? Did you step or pee on a critter?" Ty's face light up in delight.

"No," I gasped and heaved.

"Did something bite you?" He bent down to look at my leg.

"Call Hank Sharp!" I couldn't stop screaming. "I nearly peed on Ranger Corbin Ashbrook."

CHAPTER 1

"Welcome to Happy Trails Campground and to our party." If I'd said it once, I'd said it a million times today. "Here is our brochure. We cater to campers with tents, pop-ups, fifth wheels, and vans." I smiled and shrugged. "We cater to all. Even the ones who need a place to sleep." I flipped open the brochure to show the young couple who'd come to the monthly party we hosted. "We have cute bungalows that range in size and need. Are you here for the long Labor Day weekend?"

"We've been wanting to do the whole Appalachian Trail, but figured we'd better do some smaller hiking first." There was an eager look on the young woman's face that I'd seen before. "We have a couple of days off and thought we'd drive down and check it all out."

"I'm the hiker. Beth here, well. . ." The young man's eyes squinted at her as he smiled. "She's more along the lines of a glamper."

"Oh, silly." Beth rolled her eyes and put her hand on his chest. "Chuck doesn't give me much credit. Don't get me wrong. I love room service and a good spa, but if we are going to get married, I'd better start doing something he likes."

"Then Happy Trails is for you." I looked between them. "The Appalachian Plateau goes right through the Daniel Boone National Forest." I pointed towards the lake. "I know you can't see it now because of all the people gathered around the band, but right beyond the tree line is the start of a beautiful five-mile hike. It's maybe one step above a beginner, but it will bring you to an amazing waterfall."

"Beth?" Chuck put his hands out. "It's up to you. A bungalow or the bed and breakfast downtown?"

The door of the office swung open. Dottie Swaggert's unlit cigarette bounced between her dry lips. She pushed her hands up in her short red hair, fluffing it out a little.

"I'm sorry to bother you, Mae. Someone's on the phone about the last bungalow for rent. I told them the fee and they insisted on talking to the owner." Her brows cocked. "I told them that you was busy with the party, but they insisted and if I know you..." She looked between Chuck and Beth. "Trust me, I know her. You'd want me to come get you."

Dottie held the portable phone.

"You only have one bungalow left for rent?" Chuck asked, his brows knitted together with worry.

"I do. We were totally booked, but due to some unforeseen circumstances, someone cancelled at the last minute." I took a few steps closer to Dottie to get the phone. "Thanks to social media and all those hashtags, we usually fill a vacancy within minutes of a cancellation."

It was true. For years I'd said I'd never get on social media. That was before I became the owner of Happy Trails Campground in Normal, Kentucky, sight unseen. Once I did see it. . . Boy howdy. It'd needed a redo more than I needed a life do-over. That's why me and Happy Trails were perfect for each other. I had discovered not only myself, but that social media could help a business better than any other type of marketing.

Just as I extended my arm to grab the phone, Beth began to stutter and mumble something.

"What?" I asked and leaned in an ear.

"We'll take it." Beth bounced on her toes and clasped her hands together. She looked at Chuck. "Right?" The tone in her voice didn't seem so sure.

"Right!" Chuck jumped at the chance. Beth threw her arms around Chuck.

"Dottie, can you please tell the person on the phone the bungalow is no longer available?" I asked her, knowing that she'd set this whole thing up. It wasn't the first time someone was on the fence about renting either a lot or a bungalow and Dottie pulled the old someone wants to rent now trick, making it a tad more urgent for Chuck and Beth to say yes.

All of us turned around when we heard quick toots of a car horn followed by a couple of long beeps from a fast-paced carload of people driving up from the entrance of the campground.

"Woo hoo!" said a young man with a big smile, dangling his arm out the window. There was a beer in the grip of his hand and a flashy watch on his wrist. The car came to an abrupt stop.

I sucked in a deep breath and let out a slight moan. This wasn't the impression I wanted Beth and Chuck to have on their first camping experience.

"Guys. Settle down," said the driver, who was also a

young man, as he tried to calm down the others after they all started to celebrate their arrival. He got out of the car and stuck his head back through the driver's side window to give the group one last scolding.

"Why don't we go ahead and get you registered." I gestured for Beth and Chuck to follow me into the office. I glanced at Dottie. "Why don't you see what they want," I suggested, knowing she didn't take a whole lot of bull and would send them on their way.

"I'll be more than happy to do that." The look of satisfaction on her face made me smile.

"Sorry about that." I wanted to make sure Chuck and Beth knew Happy Trails was a nice, relaxing place with fun, not rowdy, guests. There was an immediate need for me to apologize.

The office space wasn't big. It was just a small, open space with metal files and two desks. There was a big window on each wall, which made it easy for us to see all sides of the campground while we were in there.

"Here are some papers I need you to fill out." I handed them a clipboard with all the papers and a pen tied around the metal clip with a piece of yarn. "This one is for the rental agreement. It has all the particulars about trash and how you need to leave things after you check out." I flipped through each page as I pointed out what they were. "I'll need a copy of your license for safety purposes if you are going to be going hiking. Not that we've lost a hiker," I assured them.

My eyes glanced over their shoulders and I could see that the car of boys had emptied out. All of them were standing with their arms crossed, arguing with Dottie.

"While you fill those out, I'm going to go check on Dottie." I didn't want those boys to bring any undue attention to the campground, especially since they were here during our monthly themed party. I shut the door behind me. "Is everything okay out here?"

"I want to see the owner and she won't let us," the one I recognized as the driver told me. "I've had a reservation for me and my friends for months. It's my bachelor weekend."

"They don't have their reservation number." Dottie's eyes lowered. She wasn't too trusting of people and it made her a great office manager.

"William Hinson." I stuck my arm out for him to shake.

"Yes, that's me," he said with a calm voice and straightened his shoulders a little more. "Do you have our reservation?"

"I do. Remember the reservation that was booked for two weeks because we don't do middle of the week reservations for the bungalows?" I looked over at Dottie. Whoever had booked the bachelor party had reserved the bungalow way in advance. "Mr. Hinson's bride sent a few items for you and your friends ahead of time."

A couple of days ago we'd gotten a big package in the mail from William's bride-to-be. It was filled with snacks, movies, and gear for hiking and fishing.

"She did?" He grinned.

The other four boys patted his back.

"He's got a good one." I recognized the one that was flailing his arm out the car window earlier. "Jamison." He nodded at me. "My name is Jamison Todd Downey."

"I get that. I'm Mae." I wasn't about to give my full name, which was Maybelline Grant West. It wasn't uncommon for southerners to give you their full names upon introduction. The more we talked, the less rowdy they were, just excited.

"You've got these yahoos?" Dottie wasn't very forgiving

when a first impression made her cringe. I could feel the tension coming off her shoulders as they hugged her ears.

"I will take them to their bungalow while you finish up with Beth and Chuck," I said to Dottie.

It was nice to be able to team up with Dottie. She'd been the manager at Happy Trails way before I'd gotten there. I'd come to rely on her for a lot of things, but hospitality to everyone wasn't her specialty. She was fabulous at putting together parties and keeping the campground running like a well-oiled machine, but she didn't take any nonsense, which these boys seemed to have plenty of.

"Hold on a second." I told the boys and went back into the office with Dottie. "Beth and Chuck, this is Dottie. She's going to finish up getting y'all settled. You're in great hands."

They nodded eagerly and went back to filling out the paperwork. I walked over to the filing cabinet and opened the H drawer for Hinson to find William's reservation. There was a lot of paperwork and computer work to be done. It was best to get him to fill out the paperwork at the bungalow he'd rented instead of bringing him in the office with the couple.

"They might need a starter camping kit," I said to Dottie about the couple. I grabbed the key to the bungalow with four bedrooms where we'd stuck William and his friends plus a clipboard full of paperwork. "I'm not sure if they've got towels and things either."

When I finally got settled into being owner of Happy Trails, I realized many campers forget everyday things like toothbrushes, towels, and other personal hygiene items. That's when I came up with the idea to put together camper packs. We offered them at several different prices, depending on what was included. We also rented fishing and hiking supplies, including poles, backpacks, and picnic baskets.

I partnered with a few of the local shops in Normal, offering their items in different baskets. The Cookie Crumble Bakery's delicious chocolate chip cookies that were the size of my head were a hit along with coffee from the new coffeehouse in town.

Gert Hobson, owner of The Trails Coffee Shop, put together packages of coffee and filters for the rental campers and the bungalows. She also supplies the complimentary coffee I offer in the morning at the recreation center on the campground. Anytime I could help a local store, I did.

"Are you good?" I asked Dottie before I left to get the boys settled into their bungalow. I could see there was still some tension about the Hinson bachelor party.

"I'm fine." She didn't sound fine, but there wasn't any way to question her in front of customers, so I left and decided I'd take it up with her later.

"Why don't you head on down to Bungalow Five. I'll be right behind you." I put the items in the golf cart. The bungalows were located at the farthest end of the campground and more nestled into the woods while the concrete pads for the campers were out in the open, with a few lots that had tree coverage.

"Thank you." William took the keys. "Boys, back in the car." He lifted his arm in the air and twirled his finger around. They all piled in.

"Y'all sure do have some fancy watches." I noticed they all looked alike.

"I got them for all the groomsmen as their present for being in my wedding. They even have their initials engraved on the back." He flipped his off and showed me.

Southerners loved to put their initials on everything. Including shower curtains.

"Be sure you adhere to the fifteen mile an hour speed limit," I warned him. That was something I'd definitely kick them out of the campground for. We had many families with children and pets, including my Fifi. "I'll be right behind you. First I have to stop by my own camper."

They took off in their car and I got into the golf cart. Fall in Love with Kentucky was the theme of the month and honored Labor Day. Dottie loved how she incorporated the fall season in the name. It was one of the most popular seasons at the Daniel Boone National Park. She'd used different camping items to decorate. Canoes, a couple of tents decorated with bobbers and plastic fish, checkered tablecloths, bourbon barrels, and campfires going with a s'more station.

The recreation center had games for everyone including cornhole, horseshoes, and ladder golf, just to name a few. Blue Ethel and the Adolescent Farm Boys were on the stage singing their hearts out while they played the banjo, guitar, harmonica, and the jug. It was a true bluegrass band that went nicely with the theme.

There were cornstalks with bales of hay all over the place for extra seating. Pumpkins, gourds, and colorful mums filled old tobacco baskets and planters of different sizes.

I pushed down the gas pedal on the golf cart to head on down to my camper. The fresh air filled my lungs and spread a happiness through my body. A few months ago, I'd never imagined myself here, much less the owner. When I found out I was the owner, I'd decided I was going to sell it as fast as I could find a buyer. As I started to get to know the small, southern town of Normal, the more I began to enjoy the slow-paced life surrounded by nature. It was food for the soul and when a buyer did come along, there was no way I could even imagine letting it go. Dottie Swaggert and I, along with many members of the community, had brought Happy Trails back to what it used to be.

For me. . .it was home.

CHAPTER 2

"Hey there, little mama," I bent down to pet Fifi, my pregnant poodle, when I walked into my camper. "I thought you might need to go potty."

My eyes dipped down on the corners when I had to help her up. She was so big with the three little ones that she had a hard time holding her tinkle and waddled when she walked. There were times when I didn't let her out fast enough and she'd pottied on the floor. I never cussed her, but I did call Ethel Biddle's brown and white pug, Rosco, a few colorful words.

Fifi nudged me with her nose. I picked her up and took her outside to do her business.

"There you are." Ty Randal was walking in front of the camper. He had on a pair of khaki shorts and a pinstriped blue button up. It was the strange time of day when the sun was setting and the campground was blanketed with a cool breeze. "I've not seen you all day. Nice evening we are having."

"It is gorgeous. We had a few late arrivals. I thought Dottie needed some help." My heart did a pitter-patter when his blue eyes looked at me. I took advantage of the effects of a nice deep breath of cool air to get me refocused.

"The rowdy boys." He looked towards the bungalows.

"You heard already?" It was no secret gossip traveled fast around here, but within a couple of minutes?

"The deaf could hear them hooting and hollering all the way down the road." He ran his hand through his hair. "I hope they don't cause trouble."

"Me too." Although I didn't think the group was terrible, it was a bachelor party and there was a nigglin' feeling in my gut they were going to be a little rowdier than our normal group. "They are only here for three days."

"It's going to be a beautiful three days for the holiday weekend." He flashed that gorgeous white smile. "Do you think babies will make it even better?"

"She's about to pop." I looked over at Fifi. She was struggling to make it over to a grassy area. "She's about sixty-three days, which means any day now."

The veterinarian told me Fifi's pregnancy would last around 9 weeks. She was already a few days' pregnant when Tammy Jo Bentley had surrendered the pregnant four-year-old to me. Long story short, I'd done some cleaning for Tammy Jo as a side hustle. When she was held in jail under suspicion of murder, she picked me of all people to take care of Fifi. I didn't know a thing about dogs - barely did now - but she was in my care. I couldn't watch her every move so I let Ty's little brother, Timmy, take her for walks and play with her while I did things around the campground.

It just so happened Ethel and her band were here for another monthly party and she brought Rosco. Timmy thought the two dogs were playing - they obviously weren't. The problem was that Fifi was insured due to a long line of prestige breeding and one night at Happy Trails had changed that. Tammy Jo was beside herself and since Fifi could no longer carry on the bloodline, she was no use to Tammy. Tammy Jo dropped her off at my camper and left me no room to protest.

Long gone were the days Fifi spent at the spa; she was too busy running around the campground to worry about staying clean. The gourmet meals were long ago replaced with campfire leftovers and whatever dog food was on sale at the grocery store. But she seemed to be doing just fine. She was a happy little stinker who found a place in my entire heart, leaving just a smidge for Ty.

"I guess we better get a date in before you become a grandmother and all your time is taken." Ty's smile reached up to his eyes.

"I'd love that." This would make the fourth date we've had, but who was counting? The word date was being used very loosely here. "What were you thinking?"

"How about a nice hike to get in some fall colors before you get too busy to enjoy it?" He was always taking my needs into consideration. It was one of the things that I just adored about him.

"I think it's perfect. I have tomorrow off. How about tomorrow?" I asked.

"I've got to get through the lunch crowd at the diner first," he said.

Ty had grown up in Normal. His dad, Ron, owned the Normal Diner located downtown. Ty and his dad were chefs. Ty's mom had died of cancer, leaving Ron to care for Ty's two younger brothers. Ty was living in San Francisco, working as a head chef in a farm to table restaurant until his father's last illness, a severe burn to his hands from the fryers at the diner.

He'd always rented a yearly lot from Happy Trails and

used it as a vacation spot until he recently moved back full time. Since then, we'd been dancing around the chemistry between us by having a cocktail here, bumping into each other there, and taking a couple of walks. Nothing really big like driving in a car somewhere and that's what I meant by loosely.

"What if we make it around one p.m.? That way, dad can just do the cleanup," he suggested.

"It's perfect. Fifi will be ready to nap and I'll have my walking shoes on. I'm looking forward to enjoying a little bit of nature." Something else that took me by surprise after I moved here. I used to hate camping and nature, but now that I'd grown up a little, in my thirties, I'd grown fond of the peacefulness and time spent with myself it offered me.

There was a loud bang coming from the direction of the Bungalow Five.

"I better get them all settled in," I said to Ty as we said our goodbyes.

I got Fifi settled back into the camper and made sure all her bowls were filled before I left. We didn't need little mama hungry or thirsty. At this point, I'd fallen in love with the little rascal and I just want her to be safe during this pregnancy.

Once Fifi had laid back down, I walked down to the bungalows. There wasn't anything going on. The bachelor party and the couple weren't there and it appeared all was right with the world. I had some hope the initial excitement of the bachelor party had calmed down.

The party was in full swing. By the looks of it, the party was going to go well into the night. Even Dottie Swaggert had joined Ron Randal on the makeshift dance floor in front of the band. On the walk back over to the lake, I noticed campers were taking advantage of the pedal boats, the games near the recreation center and the food.

FROM A DISTANCE, I SAW DOTTIE GIVE A LITTLE HIGH FIVE TO Mayor Courtney Mackenzie. Dottie wasn't too fond of the mayor. She said the mayor was so crooked you couldn't tell from her tracks if she was coming or going. Whatever that meant. I'd given up trying to figure out some of the things Dottie said.

At the end of the dock, my friends from The Laundry Club were sitting on the edge with their toes dangling in the water.

Abby Fawn, the Normal County Library librarian and local Tupperware consultant, pushed her long brown hair behind her shoulder and wildly waved me over. She nudged Betts Hager and pointed towards me. Betts brushed her bangs out of her eye. She and Abby were both waving at me. Queenie French smiled when she noticed me.

Betts wore many hats. As if it wasn't hard enough to be the local preacher's wife with all the duties that came along with that job, she also cleaned houses and owned The Laundry Club.

The Laundry Club was the laundromat located downtown, but it was much more than just a bunch of washer and dryers. It'd become a place for us to hang out and visit. Betts had made it very cozy and welcoming by adding a coffee station, book club meetings, puzzles, and TVs.

They took me in when I came to town and didn't deserve the kindness they extended. They truly have been instrumental in my staying in Normal and in the success of Happy Trails.

"Your monthly parties keep getting bigger and bigger."

Betts stood up and pulled the rubber hairband from around her wrist, tugging her long wavy brown hair into a low ponytail.

"I can't take the credit." I nodded towards Abby. "If it weren't for Abby's genius marketing skills, I'd never been able to get the word out."

"Oh!" Abby leaned on one side of her hip and took her phone out. She pointed it towards me and Betts. "Smile."

Betts and I laughed and put our heads together with big smiles on both of our faces.

"Hashtag Happy Trails Campground is a place for hashtag family hashtag vacation with hashtag fun." Abby tapped away. "I've got all my social media accounts tied together so this photo will go everywhere."

"Wait! Stay there!" There was a familiar voice behind me yelling, followed by heavy footsteps. When I turned around, I saw it was Alison Gilbert.

Alison was the local reporter who wrote for the National Parks of America Magazine and the Normal Gazette. Her heavy 35mm camera hung around her neck and a big bag was strapped across her body. She was in work mode.

"Let me grab a picture for the paper." She motioned for me and Betts to stick our heads together again. "Say s'mores."

Betts and I laughed as we did what she told us to do. Slowly, she pulled the camera from her eye and left it near her cheek. I followed her eye that was looking over my shoulder. She was staring at Ranger Corbin Ashbrook, who was standing at the beginning of one of the trails along with Mayor Courtney MacKenzie.

Corbin was one of three forest rangers we had in our area of the Daniel Boone National Forest. During the campground parties, a ranger came around to make sure no one got on the trails and did crazy things after they'd been drinking. There were a lot of dangerous cliffs, drop offs, and ledges in the park. Unfortunately, each hiking season brought unexpected deaths. Luckily, we had good rangers to help keep everyone safe.

I didn't know a whole lot about Courtney, but I was happy to see her here at the party. We'd extended an invitation every month only to be met with a decline.

"Wonder what's going on over there?" Betts looked toward the trails. "Shocker." Betts's nose curled. "Looks like the Mayor has her nose in it too."

"Eeee-lection year coming up," Queenie's southern drawl pulled out the letters in her word. She pushed the red headband off her brows and up to her forehead. "She knows how to work it."

"Ugh," I groaned. "Corbin has a hold on William Hinson. He's having his bachelor party here."

"Looks like you've got your hands full." Abby lifted a brow.

"Yeah, I better get over there," I said after I noticed Alison had already high-tailed it over there, snapping photos.

Betts Hager was a true friend and hurried next to me to help. Or maybe she was there for the gossip. Either way, from the sound of the escalating voices, I could use the backup.

We rushed over as fast as our legs would go. The argument was getting louder and louder, starting to bring attention to themselves and make a scene.

"I just need a bandage," William spat with a slur. An obvious sign he'd had too much to drink. William jerked away from Corbin. "What's your problem? You can't give me a bandage?"

"William." I tried to get his attention. Out of the corner of my eye, I saw my backup had disappeared.

"*Ahem,*" Courtney cleared her throat. We made eye contact.

"Mayor," I said, since she obviously wanted me to note she was there. I'd never met the woman before.

William and Corbin were still in a little scuffle in front of us.

"I see we have a rowdy visitor to our town." Mayor pinched a no-teeth grin.

"I'm a hardworking American that pays you to hike all day." William was just getting plain nasty. "You should pay me for allowing you to work here."

"Okay." I stepped in. "Let's get you back to your bungalow." I grabbed William's arm. "I'm sorry, Corbin."

"I've done warned him and his friends." Corbin gave Betts an odd look when she shoved a napkin with a cookie on it in his face. "Peanut butter?"

"Yes. One of the church ladies made it especially for today," Betts spoke with pride.

"I'm allergic to peanuts," Corbin said and his jaw loosened. He turned back to me. "I'm not going to haul him in, but you need to keep an eye on that bunch."

I looked at Betts and mouthed "thank you" because I wasn't sure if it was her that changed Corbin's mind with the cookie or because she was the preacher's wife. Either way, I truly appreciated it.

Alison continued to snap away.

"Seriously, Alison?" I asked. "Are you really wanting photos of this? It doesn't look good for the community and if you print those, people might not want to come visit or vacation."

"Mae, don't be ridiculous," the mayor said with a laughter. Her jaw tensed. Her eyes narrowed. "Corbin knows this is our busy season."

"Yes, Mayor. I do, but I have a job to do and if I have to shut down this part of the Daniel Boone National Park, I will," Corbin said.

I jerked my head up to look at him. Courtney sucked in a deep breath, gave her most perfect smile, and her chest slowly went down as I watched her regain her composure.

"It's so much more than that." Courtney and Corbin gave each other a look that told me he knew what she was talking about.

"I'm going back with my friends. I'm getting married." William winced after he tried to jerk away from my grip where my nails were digging into him.

"No. You're going to get some sleep." It wasn't negotiable.

"Code W." Corbin said a little too loud, probably wanting to get the last word in since a crowd had gathered to see what all the excitement was about.

"Code W?" William's head twisted around as I dragged him forward.

"Yeah! Code Wimp is what we call hikers like you." Corbin laughed harder.

"This is going to happen all the time if you shut down the entire park." I heard Alison say to Corbin. "Seriously? A drought?"

"Alison, leave it alone. Yep. There you go. Reporting on something that's not taken place yet." Corbin was in a bad mood and he wasn't going to leave anyone alone that approached him, but the word shutdown did catch my attention.

If they shut down the park we'd be in a world of hurt.

"Come on," William jerked away. "Let me go with my friends," he whined.

I pointed to the bungalow.

"If you want to be kicked out and end your bachelor party right now, go ahead. But if you want a second chance, then you better go sleep it off," I said.

He shuffled along side of me with his head hung.

"Listen," I said after we'd finally made it to the door of the bungalow. "There are no more chances. We are a family campground. We don't want rowdy and I told your fiancée that when she booked your stay. If you can't behave like a grown man, I suggest you take your friends elsewhere."

I wasn't good at kicking people out, but it was for his own good.

"It can be dangerous up here if you can't control your liquor intake." I opened the door for him. "Now, you go in there and sleep this off. I'm going to grab you some food and bring it back."

With his chin still hanging down, he finally went into the bungalow.

"Listen, don't bring me any food. I think I just want to sleep like you said." He shut the door.

On my way back to the party, I could see Dottie had now joined the conversation between Alison and Corbin. Alison wasn't going to give up. She was relentless. I knew. She'd interviewed me for the National Parks Magazine one time and she dug into my past life where I'd gone through the Kentucky foster care system after a horrible home fire had taken the lives of my parents.

It was a life I had left behind the minute I turned eighteen years old. It was funny how I'd gotten back to Kentucky and no shutdown was going to destroy it. Especially because of a drought.

CHAPTER 3

"Are you sure you're okay?" I looked down at Fifi as I poured myself the first cup of coffee of the morning.

There would be more cups to follow. I was always exhausted the day after a monthly themed party. As the owner of the campground, I stayed up until the last person left to make sure all the campfires were out and the food was put away, which was well past my bedtime. We didn't need any fires, since the forest rangers were predicting a drought. We didn't need extra critters tearing up the food table. We had enough animals around here and Fifi was about all I could handle at this moment.

"I don't want to leave you here today if you don't feel good," I said into those sweet, big brown eyes.

Her tail wiggled along with the entire back end. She was fine and happy, which made me happy.

"You were a little restless," I told her as I filled up her bowl with kibble. "Are you about to have your babies?"

The past couple of nights, she'd seem really irritable and unable to get comfortable, keeping us both up. From all the research I'd done, I knew she'd become a little more fidgety as she got closer to having her babies.

A few more pats on the head and kisses, I had my full thermos of coffee and was out the door.

A blurred, blood-red sun rose above the tree line on the horizon. There was a slight breeze blowing a few of the leaves that'd fallen off a little too early for the fall. There was a hint of cooler weather in the air and it was almost time to put a sweater on over short sleeves. Or a comfy sweatshirt.

As if the weather and the beautifully painted sky weren't enough to fill me full of joy, the hiking date I had with Ty put a little more giddy-up in my step. I glanced back at his camper. His car was gone, though I knew it would be since he had to get up really early to open the diner.

Dottie Swaggert was already at her desk filling in all the reservation requests we'd gotten out of yesterday's party. It was one reason we did the party.

"Woooweee doggie, we got us a lot of requests." She tapped the computer monitor. "Of course, we are booked for most of the requested dates, but I'm adding them to the mailing list and the email distribution list and giving them options for future dates."

"Your party turned out great," I gushed on my way over to my desk where I put my coffee down before I went to look over her shoulder.

"This is gonna keep me busier than a funeral home fan during the month of July." She nodded.

Dottie always had a way with words and she always made me smile.

"Say, did you overhear anything about a drought in our part of the Park?" I asked referring to what I'd overheard from Alison yesterday when she asked Corbin about shutting down our part of the park.

"There's always rumblings." Dottie looked up from her computer. She leaned back in her chair, planting her elbows on the armrests. "Why?"

"Yesterday Alison said something about how that sort of situation with William would happen all the time." When I said his name, Dottie rolled her eyes.

"What does that mean?" Dottie's head turned as her eyes lowered as if she were thinking about it.

"I guess if they close our trails, then people will still hike and get even more rowdy if there's no ranger on duty." I gnawed on my thoughts for a second before I shrugged it off and went over to my desk.

"No need to worry about tomorrow's problems." Dottie went back to inputting the information about potential campers into the computer. "What's on your agenda for your day off?"

"I've got to get the money to the bank from yesterday's check-ins," I said and bent down next to my desk to open up the safe where we kept the money. "And. . ." I curled my bottom lip under my front teeth and smiled like a teenager in love. "I've got a hiking date at one with Ty."

The campground reservations for rentals started on Sunday and ended on Saturday, which gave Henry, the Happy Trails' handyman, only a few hours to clean the bungalows or the area around the lots to get ready for the next campers.

"Well, butter my butt and call me a biscuit." She smacked her desk so hard, I jumped. "I can't believe it. There's nothing gonna stop y'all this time."

"I figured taking off on Friday before the long weekend was better than my normal Saturday." I thumbed through some papers on the desk just to make sure everything was good for the day. Not that she couldn't get in touch with me if she needed to - I was still going to be on the property.

She was right. Every time Ty and I did make some sort of plans, something awful would happen, like his younger brother getting sick before we were going out to supper.

"It's not like we are going in a car. We didn't want to take that chance." I laughed at how ridiculous it sounded. "But we've spent some time together here and there. Nothing really alone. Not that hiking was truly alone, but sometimes being surrounded by nature could be romantic and I was willing to see if there was a little more to my initial feelings for Ty than just a physical attraction."

"Oh, honey," Dottie tsked. "There's more to you two than a physical attraction." She winked and reached next to her computer monitor to grab her box of cigarettes.

"I thought you were quitting. What happened?" I asked.

"Mind your own business." She popped out of her chair and headed straight out the door.

Instead of hounding her, I decided to grab the money to do the deposit as well as the quarterly taxes. By the time I'd get those done and taken to the bank before I put the taxes in the mail, it'd be time for me to check on Fifi and change for my hiking date with Ty.

It didn't seem like I'd been working on the deposit that long when Skip Toliver strolled in the door. Skip was the Mayor's brother and he was always trying to start new business around town that never took off.

"Hey there, May-bell-ine," he teased.

"I see you've been talking about me to Bobby Ray Bonds." I grinned at how my longtime friend, Bobby Ray, referred to me. "Just so we are clear, my real name is Maybelline, but I go by Mae."

"He's a character." Skip had that hiker look. He wore a

plaid long-sleeved shirt tucked into a pair of hunter green shorts with tall brown socks ending with a pair of hiking boots all tied up. The loose sandy blond curls that fell around his head made me swoon with jealousy. If only my curly hair would lay loosely and not in springs. "But I was getting my oil changed down at Grassel's. Joel had Bobby Ray do it and he was fast."

"Yeah, he's been fooling around with cars as long as I've known him." It was Bobby Ray who I had to thank for getting me out of Kentucky and my old life. He'd given me the money to hop on a Greyhound bus. It wasn't until a few months ago and after my interview conducted by Alison that went into the National Parks of America Magazine, Bobby Ray'd found me. I put him up in a bungalow and got him a job at Grassel's Gas Station. "He's really good at his job."

"It was him that encouraged me to come see you." Skip pulled out some business cards from his back pocket and handed me them. "I've opened up a new whitewater rafting business that actually runs along your Red Fox Trail."

The Red Fox Trail was aptly named because there were a lot of red foxes around these parts and they seemed to love that trail in the park.

"I was wondering if you wouldn't mind giving these out to your campers and maybe throwing me a bone in the social media area. I really want this business to take off." He stared at me, leaving me in a very uncomfortable position.

"Are the rapids up?" I asked. "I'd heard it's a little dry out there."

"You're talking about that drought thing?" His finger wagged back and forth between me and the window that had a clear shot of the trail's beginning. "My sister said something about that when I told her about this and I really don't think it's going to be a problem."

"It will be a problem if Corbin and the rest of the rangers decide to close down the trails around here. Bad for you and me." There was no sugarcoating it.

"It's just a rumor and don't take this the wrong way." He put his hand out in front of him. "You've not been in Normal during a drought and this isn't a drought. Sure, we had a brutal Indian Summer, but look at those trees." He pointed out the window. "They are vibrant with fall colors and they'd be brown if there was a drought."

That made sense and I'd never thought about that.

"I'll be more than happy to give those out." I lifted my hand to take them.

"The social media?" There was hope on his face.

"Let me see what I can do. I can't promise anything since I don't do that part of the business." I couldn't imagine Abby not throwing Skip a bone. Any new business to bring in tourists would help us all out.

"Great!" He put his hands together and bowed down, walking backwards towards the door. "I've got to run and get the word out. I truly appreciate it, May-bell-ine."

"Do you work seven days a week?" I noticed his hours on business card left no room for him to have a social life.

"Yes, I do. I used to have a weekly Friday night commitment, but not anymore," he said. "I'm passionate about getting this off the ground. Like you, I work all the time to do it."

"I hope we can get you some business." I waved goodbye as he walked over to the door.

Dottie and Skip passed each other on his way out and her way in.

"Was he here to campaign?" Dottie asked suspiciously.

"No. He's started another business." I handed her one of his cards. "Whitewater rafting and canoeing."

"Doesn't he watch the news?" There she went again, rolling her eyes and dismissing the card. "There's evidence of a drought."

"I thought you said you'd not heard anything about it." I reminded her.

"While you were in here playing nice with him, I did. You need to be careful who we align the campground with. Especially since he's the brother of the mayor. Some citizens aren't happy with her and they will think you are supporting her."

"Geez, Dottie. I don't even think like that." I sure hoped no one thought that.

"Anyways, I made a few phone calls and the decision from the ranger station is ultimately Corbin's decision because he's the head ranger. But, you can ask Hank about it." Her brows lifted.

"Forget it. There's no way I'm going to call Detective Sharp for a thing." It'd been a while since I'd seen Hank Sharp. He and I were like oil and vinegar. We didn't go together at all, even though I had to help him in the last two murder investigation in Normal, since I was somehow tangled up in both.

"He's a ranger too." She shrugged. "It's all about business And I'd sure hate to give back that money on your desk from tourists' security deposits."

We required a one-night stay deposit when a reservation was booked. Campers had up until one week before their reservation to get back the money if they had to cancel. The reason for the week was because it wasn't like we could call someone on the waiting list and expect them to jump in their RV to come here. They needed a few days to get their

RVs ready, take off work, and whatever else they needed to make it here. It was only fair to all parties. Clearly, with the stack of bills on my desk, the security deposit wasn't an issue.

"Forget it." I grabbed the deposit bag and put the money and slips inside. "I'll wait to see what I hear from Ty." I zipped the bag and stuck it under my arm, grabbing the keys to the Ford Escort.

"I'm just sayin'," was the last words I heard from Dottie before the door clicked behind me on my way out.

CHAPTER 4

The line inside the bank was about five people deep. It would've gone much faster if Ann Doherty wasn't talking everyone's ear off and catching up on the gossip.

"Hi, Alison," I greeted her when she walked in and suddenly was happy that Ann had the gift of gab. It would give me some time to ask Alison about her little chat with Corbin. "Did you like the party yesterday?"

"It was fun. Almost made me want to rent a bungalow until I seen you let rowdy, riffraff in." She gave me a blank stare. I wasn't sure, but I think she'd just insulted me.

I ended up putting that in the she's-having-a-bad-day file and decided to continue with why I was happy to see her.

"Yeah. That. What do you do?" I asked, smiling, and shrugged off her insult. "Anyways, I understand you're doing a piece on the drought and possible shutdown of the park."

"Who told you?" She gave me the side-eye.

"No one," I said with wide-open eyes. "I heard you say something to Corbin and then the Mayor stepped in."

"Both of them are trying to stop me from doing this article, but I just can't do that. I have a following of campers and they take my opinion very seriously. If I continue to promote Daniel Boone National Park here in Normal, it'll make me less creditable with my readers." Her brows rose and her jaw set.

"How so?" I questioned, so I could fully understand what she meant.

"I'm guessing those are deposits from reservations that were made yesterday." She looked at the deposit bag I was holding, then drew her eyes back up to me.

"A few." I admitted.

"I'm not asking you to tell me, but I assume you might have an opening, say..." her nose scrunched, "a month from now." She put her hand out. "Though I'm well aware you've been booked for months, but just as an example."

"Okay." I took a few steps closer to the teller window as the customers ahead of me finished with their business. I was only two away from Ann.

"They come here and spend all that money to bring their families on a nice vacation to Happy Trails but can't do anything in the national park because it's *closed*." She emphasized closed. "Now, some of these people work hard all year long for their vacation and save up. You're going to tell me that it's okay for the Mayor to cover that up?"

"I think she's wanting to think the best and hoping it won't happen because it can affect the economy." I didn't give the Mayor that much credit, but I was interested in hearing Alison's rebuttal.

Alison's eye narrowed. "She's only interested in getting people here so the economy is good for merchants like you to keep her in office."

"Hey, Mae. Can I help you?" Ann Doherty drew her hands up to her face and used a fingernail file on her nails.

I looked back at Alison.

Haphazardly, I gave the deposit bag to Ann. She yammered on about the Gucci bag I'd given her as a bribe during a murder investigation. Her words were just filling the extra space in my head that wasn't currently occupied by what Allison had just told me.

Even though, I hate to admit it, maybe Dottie Swaggert was right about me asking Hank Sharp. If and only if what Alison said was true, and there was an eminent shutdown due to a drought, then I was going to have to come up with a plan to add some fun activities to the campground during the shutdown so tourists wouldn't cancel their reservations. They had to be amazing events, but what?

"Yeah, yeah. Thanks." I waved goodbye to Ann after she handed me the deposit slip.

The heavy door of the bank seemed even harder to push as I flung it open, nearly knocking down Helen Pyle, the owner of Cute-icles. Cute-icles was the local nail and hair salon that everyone used but me.

"Mae West. How the heck are you?" She pulled the dark sunglasses off her face. She took a couple of chomps of her gum as she looked me over. "I'd sure love to get my hands on that hair of yours."

"If I thought you'd be able to tame this mess, I'd let you." I'd seen what'd come out of Cute-icles salon and let's just say it wasn't the same treatment my fancy salon in New York City had. It was all Normal had and the way I seen it, was if I needed something besides pulling my hair up, back, flat-ironing the heck out of it, or simply letting it spring around, I'd go to another town.

"Tame it? It'll be purring like a kitten after I'm done with you." She cackled and I found myself standing on the side-walk of downtown Normal with Helen's fingers plunged plum down to my scalp. "Hmmm. . .purrrrrrrr," she made kitten claws at my face.

"Oh, gosh, I wouldn't do that to you and take up your time." I was beginning to feel like I'd just stepped in it and by it, I meant doo-doo. "It takes hours for me to go to the salon."

"And it just so happens that I've got a cancellation tomorrow at noon. Lucky you, someone is going to be out of town for the holiday weekend." She sparkled in the autumn sun with her bright orange lipstick and orange, short-sleeved top that was bedazzled with different colored jewels and all tucked up in her mom jeans that were pulled clear up to the bottom of her boobs.

I looked at the orange tinted hair that was piled up in a mess on top of her head and almost started to cry right there in front of her. I wasn't good at telling people no. Especially since I'd tried so hard to give back to Normal and all its shops and that included Cute-icles. Plus, I didn't want to spend a Saturday trying to get my hair tame.

"And we can catch up on Fifi. I do miss that little girl." She had done Fifi's nails on a regular basis. Yep, you heard that right. Tammy Jo Bentley used to get Fifi's nails and hair done weekly.

Let's just say that I've yet to have them done and Fifi didn't seem to mind a bit.

"I've got to run, but I'll see you at noon tomorrow." She gave me the toodle-loo wave, leaving me speechless, which was hard to do.

As if I didn't have enough to worry about. Now I had to figure out how to get out of that appointment. Then the smell of cinnamon and sugar circled around my head, putting a smile on my face and Helen in the back of my mind.

A donut to hold me over until my hike with Ty was exactly what I needed. There was no way I'd planned a big breakfast this morning because the last thing I wanted to do was get into the woods with Ty and have to go number two. That wouldn't be romantic, so I'd only had the coffee, but a donut did smell good.

Christine Watson, owner of the Cookie Crumble Bakery, was just a light of sunshine. The freckles dotted along her face made her cute as a button. She had her brown hair tucked up into a hairnet and she still looked adorable.

"Mae, did you get the delivery this morning?" She looked like she was surprised to see me. "My sister was supposed to deliver them. Please tell me she did," she begged with a panicky voice.

"Yes. She did. And let me tell you they are a hit." My eyes scanned down the glass case where she had trays of donuts. "Actually, I was at the bank and I walked out. Instead of getting a big whiff of fresh fall air, I got cinnamon."

"Really?" There was delight on her face. "That's wonderful." She clapped her hands. "I just took out the cinnamon rolls and I bet you'd like one."

"One? Give me two." I held up two fingers. "You grew up in Normal, right?"

"I did." She pulled a spatula from her drawer of tools and slipped two of the cinnamon rolls in a to-go box. "These are fresh out of the oven and I don't even have them in the case yet." She handed the box to me. I put my hand in my purse to get my wallet. "No, no. Those are on me. You have no idea how many people come in here at night in need of an after-dinner treat. They tell me they are staying at Happy Trails and tasted the treats the Cookie Crumble put in the recreation center. I've gotten so much business from you."

"Thank you," I gave a grateful smile. "Business is what I was going to ask you about."

"What could I possibly do to help you? You've been thriving," she gushed and wiped her hands down her apron. She took out a metal tray and began placing the cinnamon rolls on it.

"It's my understanding that tourism slows down when the park is shut down due to a drought." I put the box up to my nose and smelled it. My mouth watered.

"Slows down? You mean stops. All business literally stops when there's a shutdown." She slid the glass door of the counter open and placed the cinnamon buns next to a tray of sugar cookies shaped like Kentucky. A blue dot on them represented the location of our small town. "Is something going on?" She popped her head over the top of the counter, her jaw dropped.

"There was some talk at the party yesterday about some sort of drought. And I just wanted to know if you'd been through one since you've lived here all your life." I wasn't sure how to make her feel better because I could tell she was very upset at the prospect of it. "It's just gossip." I waved my hand at her. "You know gossip around here. Thanks for the cinnamon rolls."

I had to get out of there before I made a bigger mess. I wasn't good at this gossip thing or at trying to figure out how I could save Happy Trails from a shutdown if I had to. Before I even left the Cookie Crumble, I heard Christine telling someone about what I'd said.

I turned around and she was huddled in the corner of the bakery with the phone up to her ear. "A shutdown," she had whispered into the phone. "Mae West. She owns the campground. She should know. I think she's dating the detective." she muttered under her breath. "I thought we were making a cookie for the mayor so we could get some of that money. This isn't good." She looked up and gave me a wave goodbye when she caught me looking at her from the corners of her eyes.

"Great. Now the town thinks I'm dating Hank," I moaned, wondering who she was telling that I said there was a shutdown coming. I shoved out the door. "This isn't going to ruin my hike with Ty," I proclaimed over the box of the cinnamon rolls.

That might not've ruined my morning but the Normal Gazette front page headline blinked like a big signal from the metal box newspaper stand. The big glass window showcased the front page. And it read: WISH FOR RAIN! SOON! Or all tourism will stop in Normal due to drought shutdown.

"Oh my gosh." I honestly couldn't believe Alison's article had made it on the front page of the Normal Gazette. Any other day there was a happy photo of a tourist doing some touristy thing.

I patted around the inside of my purse for some change to throw into the machine but came up emptyhanded. It was one of those things the debit card had changed for me. I rarely carried cash and never coins. When I glanced up, The Laundry Club was the first store I'd seen.

"Queenie will be all over this." I snapped my finger and trotted on down to see the gals.

Just like I'd predicted, Queenie was sitting at the card table just inside of the door with the paper snapped opened and her nose stuck right up in it.

There were a few customers in there doing their laundry, but I didn't pay attention to how many since I was on a mission to get a paper. Some of them were sitting on the dryer watching the television while a few more were at the puzzle table trying to piece together the five thousand-piece killer Betts had picked up at a garage sale. I wasn't so sure all the pieces were there, though she said the owners told her they were. Well, I was told that Happy Trails Campground was a thriving community before I had a real chance to see it and we all knew how that went.

"Queenie," I said in a hushed voice when she didn't even bother to look up to see who'd come in the door. There was a dingy bell and she never missed a good ding. "Queenie."

She lifted up her head and peered over the paper, her eyes big.

"I was hoping it wasn't you I saw coming down the street. I was praying it wasn't you coming in here when the bell dinged. But here you are." She slowly dragged the paper down.

"What?" I looked at the paper. The tension gathered in my forehead right about my eyes. "What does that paper say?" My eyes lowered.

"Well. . ." she hesitated. "Let's just say that your rowdy bachelor made the paper."

She folded the paper inside out to where the full article Alison had written was located and more than half the page was a chronological photo spread of the incident with William and Ranger Corbin Ashbrook. The last photo was me dragging William away.

"Grrrr." My teeth gnashed together and my nose snarled. "I'm gonna kill Alison!" I grabbed the newspaper and plunged my fists down to my side. "There's no shutdown. She's single-handedly going to turn away tourists with this one article."

Just as I sucked in a deep breath, Mayor Courtney

Mackenzie was crossing the street from Deter's Feed-N-Seed to the grassy median that was located in the middle of the one-way streets of downtown.

"What's happening there?" I asked.

"Something about the Cookie Crumble making a cookie named after the mayor that's going to be released today." Queenie shrugged and tried to tug the paper out of my grip, but that wasn't happening.

"Is that Alison Gilbert I see?" I leaned a little closer to the window and didn't even comment on the special cookie Christine and her sister had made.

"What are you thinking?" Queenie questioned.

I gave her a quick glance and without putting too much thought into it, I bolted out the door and ran across the street.

"Alison! Yoouuu-hoooo, Alison!" I yelled and flailed the paper above my head. "I've got a bone to pick with you!"

Alison bit her lip and looked away. I could tell she was trying to figure out a getaway route.

"I can run faster!" I screamed when she started to fast walk into the crowd that was gathered in front of the amphitheater.

The grassy median was in the middle of two streets along downtown. It was its own little park with an amphitheater, picnic benches, a covered space for reunions or get together, and plenty of trees. It was a perfect place to host celebrations and apparently, there was a cookie cele-bration today that was crowded with people. I was well aware that I'd gotten some attention with my demonic screaming and all the flailing I was doing, but when I saw Alison take off, I knew she knew she'd did wrong.

"Leave me alone!" Alison stood cornered in the covered

shelter. Her eyes as big as a beach ball. "Don't come any closer to me."

"You act like I'm going to harm you." I glared at her. "Or is it your guilty conscience? I don't care if you throw me under the bus, but Happy Trails? You could destroy the very thing that got this economy going."

Yeah, I was feeling that whole mama bear saying about how you can talk about me, but not my kids' thing. I never really understood that until this very moment.

"There was no other way for me to get the word out. If there's a drought, there's money in the budget to get some supplies to the area." She spoke of something I knew nothing about. "I proposed it at the last chamber meeting."

"The last chamber meeting was the luncheon for businesses," I reminded her. I didn't go because I was busy holding down the office while Dottie took the day off. The luncheons were casual and nothing was discussed there, so it wasn't a big deal to miss. Or so I thought.

"I know it was. I appealed to the businesses, but Mayor Mackenzie shut me down and fast." Alison's shoulders softened and pulled down away from her ears. She didn't seem to be in defense mode anymore. "I knew they'd listen to you if you said something and this is how I wanted to get your attention because you sure didn't say anything at your party yesterday when I yelled it out."

"It didn't go unheard," I told her. "I had to take care of the drunk guy and get him out before he ruined the party."

"Well, I know you haven't been here before in a shutdown, but it's not pretty." She tilted her head to the side, her brows rose, and she leaned in and said, "The wrong kind of people flock to the parks when they shut down because they know there's not a ranger on duty and this lets them do anything they want." She huffed. "One thing leads to another, fires are set, parks are burnt down. It's a mess."

"Exactly how can I get their attention?" I asked, because what she said couldn't happen.

"You singlehandedly helped the economy. This will take it down. Trust me." She sucked in a big deep breath. Her eyes slid past my shoulder. I turned my head to see what she was staring at. It was Mayor Mackenzie, smiling and shaking hands. "It'll all come out soon."

There was a tone in her voice that told me this was something much more than just a shutdown due to a drought. When I turned back around, Alison had somehow slipped away without me even noticing. Unfortunately, Detective Hank Sharp was coming my way. When we met eye contact, I knew I couldn't do a Houdini act like Alison.

"Well, well, well, if it's not Mae West." There was a glint in his green eyes. He held out a napkin with a couple of cookies on it. The napkin had the Cookie Crumble logo on it. The logo looked like a doily, with "Cookie Crumble" in the middle, the outline of a cupcake below it, and the outline of a donut below it. "I'll share."

And of course I took it.

"Thanks." I bit down into it knowing this was just an opening for the reason he really walked over to see me. "Why are you being nice?"

"Are you saying that I'm not nice?" His eyes lowered, the fall sunlight beaming down on his nicely combed black hair and casting a mysterious shadow down his face.

"I'm just saying that you're being extra nice sharing your cookie." It was suspicious. Not that we didn't like each other, it was that our paths seemed to cross only when there was, well, a murder. "Is someone dead?"

"What?" He laughed. "If there was, do you think. . ."

"Okay, what do you want?" I stopped him because it wasn't a good idea to get into a fussing match with him.

"What were you and Alison talking about?" He finally asked.

"So, you're spying on me now?" I asked and shoved the rest of the cookie in my mouth, biting down into a small peanut butter morsel. Delicious, a satisfying sigh escaped me.

"She's been stirring up a lot of trouble around here lately. I've gotten a couple of complaints and I just like to keep order." He shrugged and ate the rest of his cookie.

"We were discussing me, Happy Trails, and the beautiful fall weather we are having." I took a deep inhale through my nose and released it as a smile crossed my face. He didn't appear to be too amused. "I mean these seventy-degree temps. The leaves on the trees are like a painted picture and the birds are alive with the sound of music."

"Okay, Julie Andrews." He wiped his mouth off with his napkin and put it in his pocket.

"You know Julie Andrews?" I admit to being a tad bit shocked.

"Hasn't everyone seen that goofy musical?" He shrugged and strolled past me. "If you don't tell me what she's up to, then I'll just have to keep digging myself," he nonchalantly said over his shoulder.

"Isn't it illegal to be checking on someone when they've not done a single thing wrong?" I couldn't keep my mouth shut because I knew the Mayor had probably put him up to coming over to me because she was staring right at us.

Now I was even more curious as to what Alison knew.

My phone chirped a text, bringing me out of my thoughts. I pulled it from my pocket.

Ty: Are you here? I'm a little early.

"Crap," I gasped when I noticed the time on my phone glowed it was close to twelve forty-five p.m., I had fifteen minutes to get back to the campground before our one p.m. hike date. Quickly, I texted back that I was on my way and be there shortly.

"What?" Hanks asked with a deep-set curiosity in his eyes.

"Nothing. I've got to get back to work." I didn't even bother telling him about the real reason I had to get back. I didn't feel like listening to his smart aleck remarks about Ty.

Thank goodness the campground was just a quick five-minute drive from downtown. When I pulled in, Dottie and Ty were sitting on top of one of the picnic tables near the office.

Instantly, anything I was thinking about with the Mayor, Hank, and Alison melted away. In fact, his amazing smile made me melt like a marshmallow being held over the campfire.

"Hey, there." I rolled down my window. "You going my way?"

"Nope. Just gonna sit here and wait until William Hinson shows up." Dottie took a deep inhale of her cigarette.

"What?" I threw the gear in park and jumped out of the car. "What's up with him?"

"William." She duck billed her lips and as if there were a string attached to her eyebrows, they lifted to heaven. "Apparently, after you tucked him in yesterday, he took off."

"The guys said they waited for him all night because they were headed to the city for the titty bar." By city Dottie meant Lexington and by titty bar. . .well, that's a little self-explanatory. "They went without him. Got back this morning and he still hasn't been there."

"Did you call the ranger station?" I asked.

"Yep. I talked to Corbin. He said he'd be out. Over there's his Jeep." She pointed the cigarette towards the tree line where he'd taken the liberty to park in the grass at the front of a trail. "Not sure what time he got here because I was busy distributing the firewood for tonight's cookout," she referred to the event where all the campers make a fire and cook something different for all the other campers to walk around and taste. It's a lot of fun, but it won't be tonight if William didn't show up.

I gnawed the inside of my jaw and looked between the Jeep and Ty.

"I know what you're thinking." Ty pushed off the top of the picnic table to stand. He had on a pair of navy shorts, white t-shirt, and hiking boots. "We can go on the trail. I know you are itching to help."

"You're the best." I turned back to the car. "Do you want to go with me so I can get my clothes changed or do you want to stay here?"

"I'll go with you so I can see Fifi." He was a sucker for her. They'd instantly bonded when I was babysitting her before she came to live with me full time. "Ready?"

"Yeah." I forced a smile. There was something deep down that really bugged me about William missing.

Before we got into the car, I scanned the tree line and the entrance to the Red Fox Trail, the trail William's friend thought he'd hiked.

"You're thinking something," Ty said after he shut the passenger car door.

"I'm worried about my camper who is all of a sudden missing." I put the car in drive and drove around the lake. "I want to stop by the bungalow and check on the guys. I feel like it's my duty since I'm the owner."

The bungalows were nestled in the far back of the campground in a whole bunch of huge oak trees.

"Corbin will find him. He's probably passed out along the trail somewhere and his friends have no clue where they are or what they're doing." Ty didn't make me feel better, but he was right.

I'd been living here about four months and I barely knew my way around the campground, much less the trails. It was something that came with time and experience. These guys truly didn't look like hikers or campers with their fancy equipment and brand-new hiking boots.

"Hey, there," I hollered out the window of the Escort to get their attention. "They don't look too worried," I said when I noticed they appeared to be having a liquid lunch. And I didn't mean milk or soft drinks.

"They're just celebrating." Ty snickered.

"Without the groom." I sighed and opened the door. "Have you heard from William?"

"No," the one who was hanging out the window when they first pulled into Happy Trails answered me while the rest just looked at me.

"I'm Mae. The owner." I stuck my hand out.

"I'm Jamison." He shook my hand with a very solid grip. "I'm the best man. I called Penelope to see if she's heard from him. But she hasn't."

"Is Penelope his fiancé?" I asked. He nodded. "Did he have a cell phone?"

"Yeah. It's in there charging." He pointed to the bungalow. The page of the paper with William and Corbin fighting in the newspaper was taped on the front door of the bungalow. "We went out looking for him, but decided we'd better tell your manager, Dottie, instead of us getting lost."

"To clarify," I had to get all the facts. "When you guys got back from hiking, he wasn't here. Or was he here but left?"

"Not here. He left the trail because he cut his hand. He was coming back to get a bandage and according to the newspaper, he got into a fight with that cop." He smiled. "William is always creating chaos."

"I see that you've decided to post the newspaper article on the door." My brows lifted.

"Yeah. We are going to take it with us to show everyone at the reception during our portion of the speeches." He shrugged with a laugh. "We think it'll be funny."

"Yeah, well. I don't want any of you back on the trails. Got it, Jamison?" I didn't bother waiting for him to answer me. "Or you're going to be responsible for this group. Until we find William, you're locked in right here." I stomped my foot in the grass.

"Yes, Ma'am." He saluted me. "He'll show up. He always does."

"What does that mean?" I asked.

"You know." He winked. Chills ran up my spine. "Getting married, tying a last notch on his belt. Probably with a local."

"Let's hope that's the case." I couldn't believe them. They were awful friends. I turned around and headed back to the car and slammed the door when I got in. "They are awful. They think he's having a last fling, a one-night stand with a local."

"He could be," Ty said.

"Really?" I gripped the wheel and slowly turned into the concrete pad where my camper was located. "That's terrible."

"I'm not saying it's something to be proud of. I'm just saying that it's truly possible. I know guys who did that before they got married." He looked over at me. "Guys stink."

"I know," I said sarcastically. "The last thing we need for publicity is if a camper goes missing on top of the shutdown."

We got out of the car. I threw the flamingo key ring over top of the car while I got the deposit slip and bag from the back seat. I completely forgot to put those in the office when I first pulled in.

He already had the door unlocked and Fifi out to potty.

"Poor, baby." Ty used his best baby voice. "She looks miserable," he noted.

"She should go into labor any day now." I bent down when she heard me and waddled towards me as fast as her little legs would carry that big belly with her tail wagging. "I think I might take her to get her groomed after she has the babies."

"A new mom does like to get pampered," Ty joked. He walked over. "Why don't you go on in and get changed. I'll watch her."

"You're the best." I took him up on his offer and couldn't help but think if this hike was going to lead to a romantic kiss. A moment I'd been dreaming of.

After I dressed in a Happy Trails short-sleeved shirt and a pair of shorts, I laced up my hiking boots that were as new as the bachelor party boys'. Quickly, I sprayed myself with bug spray and refilled Fifi's bowl with some extra kibble. Little mama was going to need all the energy her little body could muster up while in delivery.

"Ready?" Ty walked in, carrying Fifi. She was panting. "I wish she'd have these babies."

"Me too." I reached into the cabinet underneath the sink and took a treat from the box. "Sweet baby girl."

She snatched it out of my fingers before Ty even put her on the ground.

"I'd say she's happy." We watched as she gobbled up the treat and made her way over to her bowl. "Let's go."

"Got the keys." He dangled the flamingo key ring from his finger. "I thought we could just walk down."

"Sounds good." I left the deposit bag on the counter so I wouldn't forget to take it to the office later. Even though it was my afternoon off, I never really was off. Somehow, I'd always made it back to the office at some point.

I wasn't complaining. Life as the owner of Happy Trails was pretty simple life. Well, as long as all the lots were rented. The bungalows were just a bonus. And with William missing and a drought, I wasn't ready to give up the simple life.

We talked about his dad and his brothers. His dad had really cut back at the diner. It was Ty's younger brother's senior year. His dad had been real involved with him and all the stuff that went along with graduating high school. Plus, preparing him for his last baseball season with the high school by getting him into batting lessons. Then there was his youngest brother, Timmy. Ron had joined the PTA at the elementary school. I didn't know much about his family and I loved hearing him talk about them.

"I truly don't take advantage of living here." I couldn't get enough of the fresh air that the Daniel Boone National Forest gave to the world. "I mean, smell that."

We stopped. I put my hands on my hips and lifted my chin in the air, taking a deep breath. My lungs expanded and released, leaving a long deep sigh as my lips curled into a smile.

"I smell the pines a lot during this time of the year." He held out his canteen for me to take a drink. "Keep hydrated.

Even though it's shaded and feels really cool, your body is working harder than you think."

I took a drink and handed it back to him.

"Thank you." I gulped when our fingers touched. He entwined his with mine and tugged me closer to him. Our eyes met and my heart rendered tenderness in his gaze. The prolonged anticipation of kissing him was almost unbearable.

"May I kiss you?"

Did he just ask for permission to kiss me? My mind reeled. He was a true southern gentleman.

"I couldn't think of anything . . ." I said before he bent his head down, his mouth covering mine.

He deepened the kiss, showing his eager side and that excited me. It'd been a long time since I'd kissed someone. His lips demanded more and more time of mine as his hand drew down my face and around my neck. He dropped my hand and put it up to my face with his other hand, cradling my face.

My body tingled all over. Or maybe it was the fact I needed to pee-pee. I was willing to hold it until this amazing first kiss was over.

There was a crack of some branches, pulling us apart. We stood still when we noticed a five-point buck gallop out of the park and cross our path.

"Beautiful." I watched in amazement.

"Yes, you are." Ty pulled me close to him as we watched the buck bounce away.

"Let's finish our hike," I suggested so we could get done and back to the camper. I had other things on my mind. "So we can get back to my place."

Ty was hiking ahead of me. He'd picked up the pace.

He was so cute. He would kick sticks or rocks off the trail

so I wouldn't trip. He was very aware of those little things that I'd never thought of.

"You okay?" He turned around and asked when he noticed I wasn't walking as fast as he was.

"I've got to go potty." My brows frowned.

"One or two?" He held up his fingers.

"One!" I yelled, it echoed.

"Just go right there behind the tree. Not too far off the trail. And watch out for poison ivy. And hurry. We are almost done." He smiled. "Then we can go to your place."

"Just to check on Fifi," I joked.

"Yep." He snapped his fingers. "That's exactly what I was thinking."

"I bet you were," I teased and headed back into the wooded area, watching my step. I didn't want to step on any critters, like a snake.

"I'm lucky I didn't have sisters. My parents and I used to hike all of these trails." I could hear him opening up about his family. He rarely talked about his mom. "You would've loved my mom. She would've loved you. I mean, you're really girly but can hang with the guys when you want to."

The more he talked, the harder it was for me to concentrate on the task at hand. I started to get in position, with a tree trunk against my back to steady me. Peeing on myself didn't sound like a good thing.

"Come on, Mae," I encouraged myself out of this stage fright. "You've got. . ." I looked down at the toes of my boots. "What on earth?" I leaned a little more forward to try to get a better look. "Omg! Omg!" I jumped up and took off running while pulling my shorts back up. "Omg!" I continued to scream and dropped when I made it back to the trail.

"What is wrong? Did you step or pee on a critter?" Ty's face light up in delight.

"No," I gasped and heaved.

"Did something bite you?" He bent down to look at my leg.

"Call Hank Sharp!" I couldn't stop screaming. "I nearly peed on Ranger Corbin Ashbrook."

CHAPTER 5

The minutes between the time Ty called 9-1-1 and when the first police officer arrived on the scene felt like forever, when in reality, the sound of sirens was about five minutes after he'd called.

Ty had sat me down on a rock on the other side of the trail. He stood next to me with his arms folded as the police officer the dispatcher had sent surveyed the area.

"What on earth is going on around here?" Dottie had brought the officer up to meet us on the trail. She was the second person Ty had called because we needed her to show the officer where we were and she knew these trails.

"I'm not sure." My eyes blinked several times. I rubbed my hands vigorously together and put them between my knees.

"How on earth did you find him?" she asked.

"I had to pee," I whispered and looked down the trail after we'd heard some heavy footsteps.

"Do you think he had a heat stroke?" Dottie asked.

"It's not that hot out," I said. "But I don't know. Maybe a heart attack or something."

The rustling of the trees overhead, the cracking branches, and the sounds of the forest played like an eerie tune you'd hear in a scary movie. Goosebumps covered my legs.

"Are you cold?" Ty asked and bent down to my level.

"No. I have a bad feeling." It was something I wished I could put out of my head. "The fact that Corbin, who knew these trails as well as Dottie, is dead."

"Has William shown back up?" I asked.

"Nope." Dottie's lips made an exaggerated pop.

"Where is William Hinson?" I asked.

"Very good question. I've been wondering that myself." The heavy footsteps stopped. Hank Sharp stood over me like one of the big oaks, his green eyes hiding behind a pair of Wayfarer sunglasses. His black hair was combed neatly to the side and slicked with just the right amount of gel. He wore a two-piece black suit with a blue button-down. His gun snapped in the holster around his waist. "His fiancée has been at the office all morning waiting to file a missing person report."

We all looked at him. Ty stood back up. The two men had a sketchy past that I'd not been able to uncover. The tension could be felt between the two men. Luckily the sounds of more footsteps ascended the trail. I stood. Ty took my arm as though he were helping me balance. Hank's sideway glance didn't go unnoticed. He pulled his glasses off and his eyes were fixed on Ty's hand around my forearm.

"It's probably the coroner. I've got the trail blocked off and the officer called to report that Corbin is dead." Hank shifted his weight to the front of his feet while he pulled a notebook out of his back pocket. "The officer also told me that you found Corbin. Is that correct?" He opened the suit coat and took a pen from the inside pocket, clicking the point out.

"Yes." My voice was weak. "Ahem," I cleared my dry throat and swallowed. "It was me."

Hank's face wore a not again, sort of in disbelief look.

"Mae, it appears the only times you and I interact is when we get into sticky situations. For instance, this morning when you and Alison were having that heated conversation you didn't want to tell me about." He flipped through the notebook and started to write in it. It was best to keep my mouth shut until he started in on his many questions. I'd seen this dog and pony show a couple of times. It was during those times that I'd gotten myself in more trouble instead of less.

"You saw him today?" Ty asked. "You were almost late and texted me you were at the bank."

"I talked to her during the unveiling of the Cookie Crumble's cookie honoring the mayor." Hank had a smirk on his face.

"I would've went with you." Ty was so sweet to have offered.

"It was by chance that I was in the area." I wasn't in the mood to explain to either of them why I was downtown.

Ty nostrils flared and his jaw tensed.

"You want to tell me what happened?" Hank had made enough waves with me and Ty for the moment. I couldn't help but think he'd enjoyed every minute of getting Ty's goat at my expense.

"We were hiking and..." Ty started to say.

"You two were hiking?" Hank gestured between me and Ty with his pen. "Together?"

"Yes. Together. A date." Ty's face was stern and his jaw set as he glared at Hank.

"I'm sorry." Hank stopped the interview and looked at me. "Was the text you got from Ty? Because I thought you said you had to get back to work."

I glared at him with no answer. He was really baiting Ty and I wasn't going to help reel him in.

"Go ahead and tell me what happened here while you were on your hiking date," Hank said.

"And Mae..." Ty started again, but Hank interrupted him. Again.

"I'd like Mae to tell me." Hank put his hand up in front of Ty's face, but his eyes were on me. "Mae, you found the body. Correct?"

"Corbin. His name is Corbin." I didn't want to refer to him as a body. I let out a slight gasp and threw my hand over my mouth while the coroner and his deputy packed up the black body bag with Corbin in it.

"It's okay," Ty pulled me to his chest. "I'm here."

"Mae," Hank called my name. "Do you want to do this at the station so there's not so many distractions?"

I wanted to believe he meant the crime scene, but by the look on his face, he clearly meant Ty.

"No. I'm sorry." I licked my lips and gained my composure. "I had to tinkle."

"You need to use the bathroom?" Hank asked.

"No. I had to pee when I found Corbin." It reminded that I never went to the bathroom, bringing it to my attention that I still had to pee.

"You peed on him?" Hank brows lifted.

"Is that necessary?" Ty spoke up.

"It is if her DNA is on him. Yes, Ty. Let me do my job or you can go on back to your hike without her." Hank's tone was stern.

"No. I didn't end up going to the bathroom because

when I looked down, I saw his hand. I screamed and ran back to Ty." I sucked in a deep breath, starting to feel a little more like myself after the men carrying Corbin's body down the trail had disappeared around the curve.

"You didn't try to see what happened or touch him?" He asked.

"No." It was better to stick with single words.

"Did you touch him?" He looked at Ty.

Ty stood there with a blank look on his face.

"Did you touch him?" Hank repeated. His voice escalated with an edge of attitude.

"Oh, so you're talking to me now?" Ty questioned in a smart aleck tone. The men stood facing each other.

Hank cleared his throat.

"Yes, Ty. This is part of the investigation. There is a man dead. I need to know if you contaminated the scene?" His attitude shifted to at least tolerable and less of being a jerk.

"When Mae started screaming, I walked her way figuring it was a snake or something. She was very upset and said it was Corbin. I did walk over there and looked behind the tree. There was a body and I didn't need to know anymore than that. I didn't even see his face. I noticed the green ranger jacket and immediately called 9-1-1. After I talked to dispatch, I called Dottie to let her know that we found a body on Red Fox Trail." Ty glanced over Hank's shoulder when an officer approached from behind him.

The officer whispered something into Hank's ear. Hank gave a few nods, sending the officer back.

"What was that about?" I asked.

Hank looked at me like I had no business asking him, then he focused back on Ty.

"Why did you call Dottie?" Hank wanted to know. The sound of crunching leaves, breaking sticks, and low murmurs sucked up any tranquility the forest usually offered in the late afternoon.

"I wanted her to show the officers where we were on the trail when they got here." Ty was so smart. I'd never thought of calling her or staying with the body. I'd a hightailed it out of there if it weren't for Ty. "I had Mae sit down and calm down."

"Not that she ain't see a dead body or three," Dottie muttered under her breath. When she caught me staring at her with my nose snarled, she laughed. "If we can't laugh about it, we'd be cryin' about it."

"Did you see or talk to Corbin when you two were. . ." his chest heaved up and then down, "hiking?"

"No." I shook my head and looked at Ty for confirmation. He shook his head no too. "We decided to take this trail because we wanted to see if we could find William Hinson before I reported him missing, but apparently his fiancée is in town now."

"She is?" Dottie asked.

"Yes. She's been down at the station filling out reports and giving us photos from her phone. It's not like him not to text her or call her a few times an hour." Hank appeared to be reading from his notes. "I see that Corbin's truck was parked at the entrance of the trail. Do you know why he was here?"

"Dottie." I pointed to her.

"William Hinson, one of the campers renting a bungalow, is missing and I reported it to the ranger station," she sternly told Hank.

"William Hinson," he repeated and flipped a few pages back in his notebook. "What bungalow is he in?" Hank asked.

"Five." I held up my hand like I was some child and quickly jerked it down.

I curled up on my tiptoes to get a gander at the notes Hank was writing because it was more than just writing the number five. He gave me the side eye and drew the little pad to his chest.

"I did go and see them before we went hiking. I wanted to get some information for myself, firsthand," I said, making Hank pop his head up in curiosity. I knew that would get his attention. "They said they went to the girly bar to see if he'd gone there early because they'd had plans."

Hank and Ty gave each other what I'd call a guy look and even though there was tension between them, it did make them smile,

"Seriously?" I groaned. "Why are you asking all these questions? Was Corbin murdered?"

"When the officer came over here, upon inspection of the body, Corbin didn't have any visible signs of foul play." It was news I didn't want to hear.

A primitive grief overcame me and I sat back down to get my wits about me before I passed out.

"Detective!" The officer yelled from the crime scene with something blue dangling from his fingers.

"Listen, you don't need to hang around here." He flipped the notebook shut and shoved it in his pocket. "I'll stop by and interview each of you after I get the crime scene cleared."

Dottie, Ty and I stood there as Hank hurried back to the crime scene.

"What do you think that is?" Dottie asked.

"It looks like a sweatshirt," Ty said and put his hand out to help me stand back up. "Come on. There's nothing we can do here."

On the way down the trail, my mind was jumbled and all the words started to tumble out of my mouth.

"This is our trail." Technically, I didn't own it, but the start of the Red Fox Trail was on my property. It was my job to maintain it. Alison will get a hold of this. With this on top of this morning's article, we'll have a million cancellations.

The silence of Ty and Dottie said a lot to me. They knew I was right.

"This means one thing." I abruptly stopped and turned around, Dottie nearly knocking into me. Both of their eyes were big and round.

"Don't even say. . ." Ty slowly shook his head.

"I've got to figure out who did this before it gets out." I turned back around. "Where the hell is William Hinson?"

"That's the million-dollar question right now." Dottie hurried along side of me and pulled me close. "I think it's a great idea for us to look into this."

"Us?" I asked.

"No. No. This isn't a good idea," Ty poo-pooed the idea from behind us.

I squeezed Dottie's arm and smiled.

"Okay, dear," I said in a teasing voice.

"Dear? Great. You're not listening to me." Ty tried to hurry along side of us, but he wasn't quick enough because we'd reached the beginning of the trail, where there were police officers all over the campground.

CHAPTER 6

The campground was crawling with officers and cop cars were scattered all over. Some of the officers were sitting on the bales of hay Dottie had situated around the campground for extra seating.

The leaves on the trees swayed from the late afternoon fall breeze that was coming in from the park, a few falling down. Soon all of the trees would be bare and signs of winter would be on the way. Soon the pumpkins and gourds nestled in baskets at the end of cornstalks would be long gone and we'd be gearing up for the campers who loved to celebrate the winter season hiking in colder temperatures. Today brought on a sadness that seemed to fit the falling and bone-chilling temperatures.

There were a few campfires already started and the smell of wood burning took over the smell of death lingering in the air.

"Did you find William?" Jamison ran over with a frantic look on his face. "No one will tell me anything. They brought out a body in a black bag." His face went pale.

"No. It wasn't William. It was the ranger that he got into a fight with yesterday," I told him as I watched the door of a police cruiser open in the distance. A petite blonde in white cropped skinny pants, a pink cardigan, and pearls jumped out.

"Jamison!" she screamed, with one hand on her heart and one hand waving at him.

"Penelope," a heavy sigh escaped him.

Penelope? I watched as the two of them met in the middle, hanging onto each other.

"Who's that?" Dottie jerked the old cigarette case with the snap top out of her bra and had had lit the thing and was sucking on it before I could even answer.

"Penelope, William's fiancée." I couldn't help but notice Jamison's hands were in a place that made it appear they were just not consoling each other about their missing friend/fiancé.

Ty had walked over to another police officer he must know. I could hear them exchanging pleasantries about family members.

"No wonder William was tying one on before his wedding," Dottie said, a puff of smoke coming out with each word. "None of Harrison's friends ever consoled me like that when Harrison died."

Dottie rarely spoke about her deceased husband and I always felt it wasn't my place to ask. But she has just pushed the door wide open for me to walk through.

"Harrison went missing?" I asked.

"No, no. But still, his hands are a little too close to Miss Priss's rump and she appears not to mind." Dottie and I turned to watch a little more.

"Do you think William is dead?" Granted, I had never let

that cross my mind until now. The situation was getting more and more serious by the minute.

"He's either dead or in deep hiding." Dottie brought the cigarette up to her mouth and took another puff. "From killing Ranger Ashbrook."

"You don't think?" My jaw dropped. "I mean, I never thought for a second that William killed Corbin until you just put it in my head."

"Mae West," she tsked, dropping the cig on the ground and snuffing it out with the tip of her shoe. "The minute Hank started asking questions about whereabouts and bringing in evidence, it became clear he was suspicious. After all, Corbin Ashbrook is a fourteen-year veteran of the force and Red Fox Trail isn't the hardest hike he's ever done. Immediately that darn Alison's article popped right on in my head and been lingerin' there since." She rolled her finger around her short red hair. "Here she is, snapping away. Fitting in like all us normal people, blending in with the crowd."

Dottie had already put Alison on trial and come back with a murder verdict before we even knew if this was a murder. Her analysis was good, though.

"Gosh." I gnawed on the edge of my lip. "She did say she'd been investigating something big and it was about to come out. I wonder if. . ."

Dottie lifted her chin towards Penelope and Jamison. They appeared to be walking towards us.

"I wouldn't say she's the only suspect if Corbin was murdered," I whispered so they couldn't hear me as they got closer. "What about their friend, Mr. William Hinson?"

"It doesn't look good that he had a fight with Corbin and is all of a sudden missing." My brow rose.

I hated to think Alison would kill someone, but I'd learned real fast the motive for murder was sometimes about something very ridiculous. Not that a shutdown due to a drought was something to just roll your eyes for a business owner, but why did Alison take such a big interest in it when the newspaper wouldn't be affected too much by a shutdown. It was definitely something to look into.

"Hey, Alison." I greeted her. "News travels fast."

"I have a police scanner alert app on my phone so I can get to a scene quicker." She snapped a few more photos. "What can you tell me?"

"Nothing. We can't tell you nothin'." Dottie was quick to answer. "Here they come," she whispered about Penelope and Jamison walking over to us.

Alison didn't seem to hear, as she continued to walk around and take photos. I made a mental note to see her later since now wasn't the right time to start asking questions about what she'd meant earlier when she said there was something big that was going to come out.

I sucked in a deep breath. My eyes softened, and, with a sympathetic smile, I greeted Penelope. "Hi, Penelope, I'm Mae West. I'm very sorry we haven't found William yet. But there's no reason to believe he's not going to show up."

"Do you think he's dead up there somewhere?" Her southern accent was deep. Her blue eyes batted. She clutched her pearls with one hand and reached for Jamison with the other.

"No." I watched how easily their hands had come together. I'd expected him to give her a quick squeeze of reassurance before letting go, not a full-on, fingers entwined like they'd done it before handholding. "He was really intoxicated and I'm sure he's just sleeping it off somewhere."

"Yep, there's a lot of nooks and crannies out there to snuggle up in," Dottie said through a smile. "Like Gina Chanel's boobs down at Sugar Bears," she whispered after she'd turned her head from them.

"Are there bears in there?" Penelope's face pinched with worry as much as it could with all the filler in her forehead and cheeks.

I'd know that look anywhere. It wasn't that long ago when I lived in Manhattan and seen the same smooth skin on most of mine and Paul's friends. Even the men.

"There are bears, but they rarely come on the trail." I tried my best to assure her. My eyes followed Jamison's hand as he slid it out of Penelope's grasp and dragged a finger along her arm before settling her back into a hug and kissing her forehead.

"Don't worry. We are going to find him. This is a separate situation." He pulled away when he seen the look on my face.

Crunching leaves and some rustling from the entrance to the trail caught our attention. Hank Sharp walked out, scanning the area in front of him until he caught my eye.

"Detective," Penelope greeted him. "Does that dead man have anything to do with my William?"

"I'm not sure. Remember the article I showed you at the station?" Hank asked her. "Well, that's the ranger."

Penelope shrieked, falling right back into the arms of Jamison, who was more than ready to comfort her.

"Why don't I take Penelope into the office? I can get her a drink and have her rest until you get all of this cleaned up and out of here," I told Hank in no uncertain terms that the campground was filled with residents as well as looky-loo campers just here to see what was going on and it couldn't be good for business. "That way we can just be one less group of people in your way while you clean this up."

"That's a good idea. Penelope, we can talk in a few minutes," he said to her, but his eyes were focused on Jamison. I knew we were both thinking this was odd. It was something I'd ask him about later.

"It's just right over there." I squeezed between her and Jamison, breaking the hold he had on her and taking her by the elbow. "When is your wedding?" I asked and noticed the sizeable sparkler on her ring finger.

"Next month. I love fall weddings and he's let me plan it all." For a second, she appeared to have forgotten why she was here. "Do you think he's okay? And what do you think the detective meant when he said that William could be involved?"

"I'm sure he's okay. I've never had this happen here." Big deal if I left out the fact I'd not been here long, but she didn't need to know that. I'm here now. "I think Detective Hank is just making sure he's taking all circumstances into consideration."

"Yeah, William has caused problems here since they drove in a couple of nights ago," Dottie grumbled and opened the door to the office. "I'll grab us some food."

"That'd be great." I showed Penelope to a chair in front of my desk.

"I know William and his friends can get a little rambunctious. It's all in fun. We are the first to get married out of the group." She had a faraway look in her eye.

"I guess he and Jamison have been friends a long time." There was a little tug in my gut to start asking questions while I had her alone.

Even though Ty didn't want me to touch this case with my amazing, yet fumbled, newly found sleuthing skills, I had to be prepared for anything. Especially if my livelihood was dependent on it.

"Why are you asking about Jamison?" There was a muscle spasm in her smooth jawline.

"Isn't he the best man? I figured they've been friends a long time." I waved off the question to make her feel like she was off the hot seat.

"Yes." She eased down into the chair and crossed her ankles.

She was one of those, my brow rising at my thought. When I was growing up, most of the girls who weren't in foster homes had taken debutante lessons. Of course I didn't, but the girl next door did and she said they had a full month on how to properly sit in a chair.

"They've been lifelong friends. I'm not going to say it's not been a strain since the *situation*," she emphasized.

"Situation?" I asked.

"I forget who I'm talking to." She put her hand up to her pearls and laughed. "I don't mind telling you since I know you don't know them. But after Jamison caught his mom and William's dad having sex in their pool house, it's been a little tense." She sniffled, lifting the top of her pointer finger to under her nose. "It's been awful keeping this secret from William."

"He doesn't know?" I asked.

"No. He'd die. Jamison isn't well off like William. Jamison is from the seedier side of our town, if you know what I mean." She gulped back what appeared to be the start of some tears. "Apparently, it's been going on for years. No one knew until now."

"How did you find out?" I asked.

"It was during our couple's shower. Jamison was so

upset. I asked him why and he told me." She blinked her long lashes slowly. "He begged me not to tell William."

"Why would he tell you something so burdensome?" I asked, but after she jerked back all wide-eyed, I quickly followed up with another question. "I mean, you're getting married and it's no way to start out a marriage with a lie."

The door of the office flew open. Dottie walked in with an armful of vending machine food. She dumped the loot on my desk and pulled out a couple of cans of soda from her pants' pockets.

"We don't have any food left over from the Bible Thumpers?" I asked. "I mean, church ladies?"

There was a lot of leftovers from the party.

"These are good." She grabbed a bag of Corn Nuts and ripped them open. "Go on, grab you something." Dottie flung her finger from Penelope to the snacks.

"I've not had hot fries in a long time." Penelope scooted up on the edge of her seat. "I have to keep a good figure and all for my wedding."

"It looks like..."

"Like you can use some comfort food," I interjected because I knew Dottie was going to say something about the wedding not happening or something like that. I could see it in her eyes as she glared at me. I picked up the package and handed it to Penelope. "Here. We won't tell anyone."

I tugged Dottie to the side, with our backs to Penelope.

"Listen, something isn't right here. I think Jamison knows more than he's saying," I whispered.

"Ya think?" Dottie snorted. "He can't keep his hands off of her and I ain't so sure she doesn't mind."

A knock on the door followed quickly by the door opening made us jerk our heads apart.

"Can we come in?" Ty stood at the door with Fifi in his arms.

"A puppy!" Penelope jumped up with a ring of red around her mouth where she had shoveled in the hot fries.

"Penelope, this is my dog, Fifi." Ty had to let Fifi down when she started to wiggle around in his arms when she saw me.

"Have you been feeding her hot fries?" Penelope joked at Fifi's weight.

"No." I snickered. "She's pregnant by a pug named Rosco."

"My, oh, my." Penelope bent down. "You naughty little poodle. Going to the other side of the tracks, huh?"

Was she referring to Fifi or her situation with Jamison? I wondered. I had to tuck that question in my sleuthing folder in my head because Hank Sharp bolted through the door. He gave Penelope a second look when he saw the red ring remaining from the hot fries.

"Did you find William?" She forgot about Fifi and went over to Hank.

"No. But we did find this at the scene." He held the evidence bag in his hand and lifted it up. "Does this belong to William?"

Instantly, I recognized it was the sweatshirt the officer had held up at the scene of Corbin's demise.

"It's got a logo." He flipped the bag.

"That's the country club's logo," Penelope cried out in a gasp. "Does that mean he's. . .gone." Her shoulders fell.

"No. It means that we found it at the scene of the murder of Ranger Corbin Ashbrook, putting your fiancé at the scene." Frustration came off of Hank in waves. "This means that finding William is our number one priority because he's our person of interest in what happened to Ranger Ashbrook."

When Hank used formal names and specific terms, I knew he meant business. This didn't look good for William.

"I'm going to have to ask you to make a plea to the news media for William to turn himself in for questioning." Hank rested his hands on his hips, shifting his weight side-to-side as he waited for her response.

Dottie had her mouth all flung open, taking it all in. Ty had picked Fifi back up. And now Penelope was in tears. The tension was so thick, I knew I had to diffuse it if we were going to get anywhere.

"I've got an idea." I put my hand up to Hank when I noticed he was about to protest me even talking. "Why don't we get Penelope settled into an open camper or bungalow? Get her a hot shower and some food and we can come down to the station after that. I can give you my official statement too."

"We don't got no open bungalows or campers. We're filled to the rim." Dottie's bird-thin lips wore a scowl. "I guess she can stay with you and Fifi since you're good at taking in strays."

"That's a great idea!" I wasn't going to let Dottie get my goat. It was true. I'd taken in Bobby Ray Bond when he came to town. I had taken in Fifi. And now Penelope. "So what do you say, Hank?" I asked.

He heaved a few breaths in and out before he finally opened his mouth.

"Okay. But, if you hear from William, I expect you tell him to turn himself in and then you find out where he is and call me." Hank did have a soft side, though he wasn't showing it at this moment. He even scared me a little, though I knew better.

Penelope nodded and blinked rapidly.

"I'll see you tonight." He looked at his watch. "Can I see you outside?" He asked me.

A loud sigh escaped Ty out of frustration. His eyes narrowed to crinkled slits when I looked at him before I went with Hank outside. The first person I saw outside was Alison, talking to Jamison. She was taking notes and he was talking.

Hank rubbed a hand over the dark stubble along his jawline. I'd not noticed it until now. It gave him an edgy look that agreed with him.

"I'm only agreeing to this because I want you to keep your eyes and ears open." He gave me an unrelenting stare.

"Are you asking for my help?" I asked with a grin.

His mouth opened, then he shut it, then it opened again.

"Yes." He fiddled with the evidence bag in his hand. "I don't think you're going to let this go and somehow the last couple of times you've been involved in one of my murder cases, you've been a step ahead of me. I'd rather be right beside you on this one."

"Why, Hank Sharp, I don't know what to say." I fluttered my lashes in a joking manner.

"If I want to get into the intimate details of this case and what's going on between Jamison and Penelope, I figured you can do that girly talk." He tucked the evidence bag up under his armpit and adjusted his stance.

"You too got the impression that something funny is going on between them?" I asked. "Like a fling?"

"Did you see how he was rubbing her and then consoling her." His nose wrinkled in distaste. "I put up with that once, but never again," his words stopped me.

"Do you mean to tell me that Nicki Swaggert is the reason for the tension between you and Ty?" I completely abandoned the conversation about the investigation and barreled down the path the two men had clearly avoided.

Nicki just so happened to be the daughter of Harrison Swaggert, Dottie's deceased husband. After I'd stuck my nose in the last investigation, I'd uncovered a link between Ty and Hank from high school that had to do with Nicki. Apparently, she had both of their hearts all hog-tied up to hers but left them both. She'd recently turned up and through some misfortunate events, she'd committed a crime and was sent off to jail for a two-year term. This made me happy because I knew she'd look sickly in an orange jail uniform.

"Nicki is in jail and of no importance." He wasn't biting my line I was throwing out there. "I'm serious. This is a murder investigation and we have to find William Hinson. Got it?"

"Yep." My chin drew a big line up and then down.

"Fine. I'll see you in two hours. Two." He held up a couple of fingers. He pulled his dangling sunglasses out from his suit pocket and slipped them back on his face. "We'll get this mess cleaned up and you'll be back to normal in a few minutes."

I stood there and watched him walk away. There was an excitement rolling around my heart. It was a combination of helping on the case and the tension between us. This was where the water that is my love life got murky.

It was like I had an angel on one shoulder and a little devil on the other. On the angel shoulder was Ty. I loved how Ty was a family guy. He loved Fifi and had such amazing manners. On the devil shoulder was Hank. The tough exterior. The manly good looks. And the edginess and hint of danger were always appealing. He also checked on me from time to time in a no one better mess with me way and it made my motor run.

And I couldn't help but wonder why every time Ty and I tried to have a moment that would move us beyond the flirtatious stage, there was a situation that jerked us apart. Clearly, there was something. There was no time to ponder what that was, I had an undercover job to do and I was going to do it. After all, it was for the good of Happy Trails and my livelihood.

CHAPTER 7

"**A**re you sure it's okay I stay here?" Penelope sat on the couch rubbing Fifi. If I did care, I wouldn't matter because Fifi seemed to be enjoying Penelope's company since she'd not stopped rubbing on her since she got here.

"Yes." I poured fresh coffee into two mugs and handed her one. The pumpkin spice and cinnamon blend was perfect for a fall night, especially one that'd gotten much chillier as the day had gone on. And I wasn't just referring to the weather.

"It might be a little tight in here, but we will manage. I'm sure William will be back anytime." I pushed a strand of my curly hair behind my ear, remembering my appointment at Cute-icles tomorrow and wondering if William wasn't back that it'd make a good excuse not to go.

"Do you think?" Penelope's perfectly waxed brows lifted with a bit of hope twinkling in her eyes. "You don't think he had anything to do with that ranger getting killed?"

"Let's just say that it doesn't look good that he had an open fight with Corbin yesterday and the newspaper printed it." I held the cup of coffee with both hands. "Now that he's missing, it makes him look there's something fishy."

"I'm so worried," she said.

"Maybe I can help." I was laying the ground work for my first step into the investigation. "I've been able to help the police with a couple cases, so why don't I try my hand at finding William?"

When I'd talked to Detective Hank Sharp, I got the distinct impression that Corbin's death and William's disappearance were connected. I wasn't so sure. From an outsider who knew nothing about Penelope, William, or Jamison, and if I'd walked up on the scene yesterday where Jamison had been consoling Penelope, I'd thought they were an item. Of course, my mind went there. This could possibly be two separate cases. Jamison was as in love with Penelope as she was with him.

"Who planned the bachelor party?" I asked. "I mean, it's not like we get a lot of those here. We are a family campground."

"Jamison. He said what better way to bond as a group of men than in the woods." She smiled. "He's always been so nice to William and wanting to keep the friends together."

I bet he does, I thought and then thought some more about how Jamison might've thought it would be easy to get rid of William in the Daniel Boone National Park after they got him all drunked up. Most accidental deaths in the park had to do with excessive drinking and falling off a cliff. Easy way to cover a murder if you asked me.

"Has William ever been camping?" I asked.

"Are you kidding?" She laughed and took a drink of her coffee. She rubbed her free hand along Fifi's belly since Fifi had turned over on her back with her little legs sticking up in the air. "We did go to Arizona once and stayed in a tent that had a king size bed, bathroom, and tent service."

"Glamping." I winked, trying to keep the conversation light so she'd continue to tell me about their life. "Did Jamison go to that with you?"

"He goes a lot of places with us." She shifted and didn't make eye contact.

"I know you said William is the first to get married, but does Jamison have a girlfriend?" I asked.

"No." She lifted her head, her eyes hooded by her brows. She tossed her head to the side. Her hair flung over her shoulder. "I'm hungry. Do you have anything to eat?"

That was the end of that conversation. Which told me that I'd struck a nerve somewhere, yet I didn't feel like it was time to question her about Jamison and his feelings for her.

"We do have an hour before we go see Hank at the station, so we can head into town." I sat my coffee down. "Let me take Fifi out to potty and put some kibble in her bowl."

"Someone gotta go potty," she talked baby talk to Fifi and picked her up. "I can help."

"Sure." I walked over to the camper door and opened it, walking down the steps to hold the door for them. "She doesn't need a leash. She's great at staying in our lot."

It was the time of the year dusk painted the sky orange around five-thirty p.m. and we were completely covered in darkness by six p.m. The only light in the sky was a sprinkling of stars and the moon. Campers were fascinated how dark it truly was since we didn't have a big city in the distance to give off light.

"Hi there," Chuck said as he walked by the camper. Beth was snuggled up to him with a big grin on her face.

"Are you two having a good time?" I asked, hoping they'd say yes and the events of the day hadn't ruined their trip.

"We've had a wonderful twenty-four hours." Beth bounced on her toes. "Yesterday we went into downtown Normal. We started at the Trails Coffee Shop for a wonderful cup of pour-over coffee."

"It was tasty." Chuck nodded.

"You can get some of their really good coffee in the recreation center in the morning.

I pointed to the building in the distance. "Gert Hobson and I are friends."

They smiled at each other.

"But do you have the muffins from the Cookie Crumble?" Beth asked with a little hope in her tone.

"As a matter of fact, we do. Same place." It was perfect how I was able to showcase the area's small businesses.

"I'm so glad we decided to stay." Beth's shoulders raised to her ears, her eyes squinted after she smiled.

"Don't forget we stopped at Sweet Smell Flower Shop because they had the most beautiful bouquet of wildflowers in the display window." Chuck didn't look quite as enthusiastic.

As they talked about how they'd gone to the Tough Nickel Thrift Shop and found a rare dish Beth's mom was going to love, I noticed Penelope had walked Fifi a few campers down.

"Where are you headed?" I asked Chuck.

"We thought we'd just take a night walk and see what was going on down there today." Chuck nodded towards the front of the campground at the entrance to Red Fox Trail.

"Do you remember the rowdy group of guys who came in after you for the bachelor party?" I asked. Both of them smiled and nodded, which was odd since they were going to leave because of them. "One of the members of the party is missing."

"Oh, no." Beth's brows formed a V. She gave the same worried look to Chuck.

"What do you mean missing?" he asked.

"He had a few too many to drink and I had put him back in the bungalow, but he must've woken up and left. His friends think that he'll be back, but we are just being cautious, you know?" I shrugged and walked with them so I could get Fifi from Penelope.

"Hey, May-bell-ine," Bobby Ray Bond, my childhood friend, came shuffling towards us. His baseball cap was on backwards, his blue mechanic overalls were spotted with oil stains, and his hands were filthy. "I hear-d there were some goin's ons around here today. Dead ranger and missing camper."

"Dead ranger?" Chuck stopped. Beth gasped.

"Yeah." Bobby Ray Bond's nose curled, he nodded. "Found on a trail."

"Nothing is official on how he died." I tried to make the situation seem less dire than it really was.

"Do they think there's a killer here? I mean, I've seen movies and there are plenty of places people can hide out there." Beth's face was now white as the moon.

"We never said anyone was killed," I clarified, trying to ease the fear that crossed her face.

"Is that Fifi? Here, Fifi!" Bobby Ray called.

She darted out of the shadow of one of the campers and came running towards us, Penelope lagged behind.

"Penelope." Beth's voice escalated. "We didn't know you and Jamison were staying here. Chuck, look. It's Penelope."

"We. . um. . ." Penelope nervously cleared her throat. "My fiancé is the one missing."

"Jamison?" Beth rushed over to Penelope. "Oh, no. We just had the best time with the two of you. What happened?"

"Well, let me know if you need anything, May-bell-ine." Bobby loved to use my real name, though I'd not gone by it in years. "I've got tomorrow off."

"Do you think you can look at the golf cart tomorrow?" I asked since Bobby Ray was a mechanic. He'd started working for Grassel's Gas Station located in downtown Normal just a few days after he'd show up to see me.

He'd seen the article where Alison Gilbert had interviewed me for the National Parks of America Magazine. It just so happened Joel Grassel needed a mechanic and there was none finer than Bobby Ray.

"First thing after my coffee." He walked on off to the bungalow where he was staying until he saved enough to get a small house in town.

Then I turned back to Penelope.

"Jamison isn't missing," her voice trailed off, her chin drew down to her chest, and she fiddled with those pretty, long, pink fingernails.

It appeared that William's dad and Jamison's mom – and Fifi and Roscoe - weren't the only ones to play on the wrong side of the tracks in their relationships.

"We better get on our way." I gave her a flat look. "Detective Hank Sharp is waiting for us."

"I don't understand," Beth blinked several times in confusion. "I thought you. . ."

"Beth, let's go." Chuck obviously knew something was off here.

"Do you understand?" Beth asked him, not letting it go. "Chuck?"

"Let's go," Chuck told her in a more demanding voice

and grabbed her by the arm to drag her along even though she was fighting and trying to turn around to look at Penelope, falling all over her feet.

"I guess you're going to want an explanation about that?" Penelope asked me.

I picked Fifi up and picked up the pace on the way back towards my camper.

"Mae?" Penelope walked briskly to keep up with me. "I can explain."

"Listen here." I quickly turned around. Fifi started to lick my face. She could tell I was upset. "I don't have time for games. I'm running a business here. You lied to the police. I thought I had a sad soon to be bride staying with me while they found her fiancé. You are nothing but a liar and I can't help but to think that you and Jamison had something to do with William's disappearance."

I darted off with one thing in mind. Get to the police station and tell Hank my theory.

"Mae, it's not like that." Penelope's voice echoed behind me.

"You're right." I stopped at the camper door and jerked it open. I turned to face her rushing towards me. "You and Jamison had a plan all this time to bring William here, get him drunk, and throw him off a cliff. Easy peasy. Best friend comforts grieving bride and they fall in love." My face contorted. "How convenient. A little too convenient if you ask me. But who is asking me?"

I shrugged. Fifi whined in my arms. I reached over the two small steps leading up into the camper and sat her on the floor inside.

"When Corbin walked up on the two of you getting rid of William, you decided to kill him. Which was perfect because William and Corbin had a very public fight yesterday, making it seem like he'd be the likely suspect to kill Corbin and then disappear." I had it all worked out in my head and it all seemed logical.

"That's not true. It's not!" She screamed, tears streaming down her face. "I love William!"

"But you liked the secret affair with his best friend more?" I asked with disgust. "You know what, I don't even want to know." I put my hand out in front of me. "You can tell Hank all of this."

"I can't," she cried ugly. Her pretty face was blotchy, with black streaks running from her eyes and her lipstick smeared. "William will kill me."

"William?" An evil laugh escaped me. "You killed him."

"No, we didn't!" She screamed and fell to her knees. "We were going to tell him after this bachelor party. But he saw us in downtown Normal when he was drunk last night. We were kissing in the town square." She sobbed. "We tried to stop him. We took off and we couldn't find him."

She continued to mutter something through her tears, but I wasn't going to let her stay with me another minute. I threw some kibble in Fifi's bowl, made sure she had water, and grabbed my purse.

"You can tell Hank." I locked the door behind me and headed to the car. "Are you coming? Or am I going to have to call the police?"

She pushed herself up to stand. Her polished look had become disheveled and broken. Like a zombie, she walked to the car. Her eyes were blank. The pretty as a picture debutante look with perfect makeup and tidy clothes had disappeared.

"Mae, you don't understand," she pleaded with me from the other side of the car, breaking the silence as we drove out of the campground.

"I understand just fine," I told her and gripped the wheel.

Downtown Normal was just a short five or so minutes from the campground, but the police station, where the detectives had their offices, was a little bit outside downtown in the business district and attached to the white courthouse. You couldn't miss the courthouse. It was the tallest building in Normal and you could see the steeple from afar.

Hank's car was butted up to the side of the building and I pulled in next to his car.

"Please, let me explain before we go in there." Her tears had dried and her eyes were wide.

I don't know what got into me but I decided to give her one shot. Maybe it was the drive over and the fact that she'd finally given me a few moments of silence so my brain could process what had come to light at the campground.

"I've been with William since high school. I would have to be some sort of club hosting wife that has to always look perfect. It's not like that with Jamison." Her face suddenly lit up after she said his name. "He doesn't care if I look like this or wear sweatpants. He loves that I eat with my fingers sometimes." Her shoulders relaxed. "I could live in a shack with him and be so happy, not the mansion William has us living in."

"Did you kill William?" I asked.

"No." She shook her head. "We ran after him. He took off. I can't find him anywhere."

"Why didn't you just break off the engagement when you realized you were in love with Jamison?" I asked.

"That's why I came here. I'd texted Jamison and told him that they couldn't go through with this weekend because I couldn't go through with the wedding. I asked him to meet in downtown Normal. I think William saw Jamison's phone when they were all hiking and he was back at the bungalow sleeping off the booze." Her chest lifted and she let out a long sigh like it felt good to get all of this out in the open. "It was like he was waiting for us to show up there." Her fingers started to tremble. "William can be a very determined man."

"Determined as in getting what he wants?" I asked.

"At any cost," her voice trailed off. "He's very controlling and quick to anger. It's another reason I didn't break off the engagement yet."

"What did Jamison say about not going through with the wedding?" I asked.

"He said we'd discuss it after we got back home. He told me he loved me and I told him I loved him. That's when we kissed and William caught us." She gulped, licked her lips, and looked over at me. "Jamison and I've been together since. Looking for him. That's when we met the couple from the campground. Jamison and I put on a happy couple face and pretended to be something we aren't. At least not yet."

"Do you think William killed Ranger Corbin Ashbrook?" I asked now knowing he can be quick tempered.

"I'd like to think he'd never hurt anyone, but I can't say he's never knocked me around." Her nose flared and she tucked her lips between her teeth as though she were biting back tears. "I'm not sure what he'd do if someone pushed him to his limits."

The door of the police station flung open. Alison Gilbert bolted out with her camera swinging around her neck.

"Alison," I opened the door and called to her.

She turned with a quick snap of her thin shoulders. A look of disbelief, rage, and frustration arranged her facial features.

"What's going on?" I asked.

"Can you believe they think I'm a suspect?" She jerked

her head back, her fists clinched at her sides. "Something about the argument Corbin and I had about the article gives me motive."

"Good." There was a look of relief on Penelope's face. "That means me and Jamison aren't suspects."

"Honey, everyone is a suspect. Including you and your boyfriend." Alison pinched her lips together.

"My fiancé, you mean." Penelope wiggled her ring finger in the air.

"No, sugar." There was all sorts of piss and vinegar in Alison's tone. "Your boyfriend. I snapped several photos around downtown yesterday for the Out and About section of the newspaper. I got an eyeful and a camera full of photos." She stuck her hand in the camera bag that was stretched across her body, reached in and took out an inhaler.

Penelope stood there stunned. Her eyes bugged opened as her lashes took long and rapid blinks.

"Seasonal allergies," Alison said after she noticed me watching her with the inhaler. She shook the bottle before taking a few quick inhales. "Stress too."

"Why on earth do you think you're a suspect?" I asked.

"Because I've been looking into this drought shutdown. Corbin has been dragging his feet on it. I found it interesting because we all know that he was a by the book kind of guy and he's never dragged his feet before." She put the inhaler in her bag and took out a file. "If you go back through the fourteen years he's been here, this is the first time he let some time pass." She flipped the file open and pointed to words that really meant nothing to me, since I'd not read the entire report. "Initially I thought it was because he was taking the thriving economy into his decision, but as I started to investigate for the story, he threatened me."

"He did?" My eyebrows dipped in a frown.

Not that I knew Corbin well, but he did come to the office a few times a week to say hello. What I did know of him, threatening somebody was not something I'd ever think he would do.

"Yeah. He said that if I wrote anything about the drought, he'd see to it that I'd be out of the national park office and out of a job. He's no different than Ardine." Her jaw tensed and she shook her head while rolling her eyes. There was frustration written all over her, including her tense stance. "The rangers are located in the same building."

"I didn't know he was like that at all. I'm assuming Ardine is his wife?" Alison confirmed with a nod. I tried to think back if I'd ever heard the girls from The Laundry Club say something about Corbin Ashbrook or his wife. "That's so hard to believe. He never appeared to be that way."

"All I can think of is that I pushed a button and was on the trail of something bigger than just the drought." Her words turned my curious side on.

"Do you have any clue what it is?" I asked.

"I have an inkling." Her brow rose.

Ahem, the sound of someone clearing their throat caught our attention. Hank Sharp was standing at the door of the station with his hands on his hips, staring at us. He pulled the sleeve of his button-down shirt up and looked at his watch. He glanced back up at us and tapped the face of the watch.

"Can I stop by and see you after this?" I asked Alison.

"Sure. I've been ordered not to leave town." She rolled her eyes so hard.

Poor Penelope was so scared that she was visibly shaking. It was like she was walking the gang plank to her death.

"For someone who is so sure she's innocent, you're

awfully nervous." I made the observation. "Hank can smell fear a mile away. If you didn't do this, I suggest you get it together."

There was a slight shift in her posture as we got closer to the door to the police station, where Hank was patiently waiting.

"Ladies, I have comfy seats for both of you. If you'll follow me." He thought he was being so funny. It didn't amuse me. We followed him into the station and through the door without having us go through the check in process at the window.

"Mae West!" Agnes Swift sat behind the window on her perch. She clapped her hands in delight. Her saggy jaws tightened slightly when she smiled. Her short grey hair was curled around her head. "I keep telling my grandson to stop letting his pride get in the way and get on over to Happy Trails to ask you out on an official date." She snickered. "Like a coffee pot is a date."

"Granny, don't you have some work to do?" Hank quickly stopped Agnes from telling me anymore.

"The coffee pot was a date?" I asked her, ignoring him. "I thought he brought me that coffee pot because he felt sorry for me since I couldn't offer him a big cup from the Keurig."

Here was my quandary in the love life department. I just adored Agnes and if Hank wasn't such a hard person, we might've gotten together long before I had my feelings for Ty.

"Mae," Hank said my name in a low southern draw that would make any gal tingle. "Seriously. I have a job to do and you aren't making it easy."

It just so happened, all the officers in the station had turned around and were watching us in amusement. Granny

Agnes must've let everyone know how she felt about me and Hank getting together.

"Who do you want to talk to first?" I asked, making it more official.

"Why don't I talk to you first," he suggested. "Penelope, you can sit right here."

Hank and I passed another interrogation room on our way back to where he was going to question me. Jamison was in there with a couple of different officers and a ranger. All of them towering over him. His face looked out the window and our eyes caught. I gulped and continued walking.

"You obviously know Jamison and Penelope are an item, right?" I asked.

"Yeah." He opened a door for me and let me walk in first. "Just sit anywhere. I let all of William's friends go home but Jamison."

He went over the piece of paper that had my statement on it from earlier. I signed it to make it an official document to be put into the case file. I couldn't help but see the evidence sheet.

"What did you collect at the scene?" I asked and watched as he sat on the edge of the seat and gathered the papers into the file.

"We got that sweatshirt. We also combed the bungalow for any DNA of William's and the DNA around the neck of the sweatshirt matches the DNA we collected from his other things. His friends did say it was his sweatshirt. There's no blood or any DNA of Corbin's on it." He rubbed his hand through his hair.

"When will the autopsy be back?" My jaw dropped.

"I'm hoping to get an initial report soon." He looked at

his watch. "We found an inhaler." The lines around his eyes deepened.

"Inhaler?" I gulped. Thoughts of Alison's story swirled in my brain.

"What? Do you know someone with an inhaler?" He asked, pulling his shoulders back into a tall, erect position.

"Just odd." I didn't answer the question. There was good reason for that. Just a few short hours ago he'd asked me to help him with the investigation. Though Alison had used the inhaler a few minutes ago, she'd not tried to cover it up and besides, I truly wanted to know what she thought she'd uncovered with Corbin. When I talked with her later tonight and I felt like she truly did kill him, I'd let Hank know she had an inhaler.

"We need to find William. Do you think she knows where he is?" He referred to Penelope.

"I don't think so, but I had no clue she and Jamison were an item until one of the tourists at the campground apparently had a good chat with them downtown." All of this was adding up to my theory that William had killed Corbin out of anger. "Penelope did say that William has a temper and I wonder if he killed Corbin after he'd gone back to the campground. Maybe he and Corbin had words and William followed him up to trail. They fought and somehow William killed Corbin?" I asked in a suggestive way since we'd yet been told the way he'd died.

"We're looking at all angles. I found out about the affair between Penelope and Jamison after I looked through Alison's photos. I recognized her instantly and then him when I went to the crime scene. They were just a little too lovey-dovey to me." Hank pulled out a couple of photos of the two lovebirds Alison had taken. "Here is one of William seeing them. He's got on the sweatshirt. So we know he'd been wearing it. The coroner said that Corbin died this morning. So where was William all night and where is he now?" He held the photo up to his face and stared at it.

"I talked to his family. They are getting his medical records, but they said he didn't use an inhaler. We are in the process of testing the DNA on it, and we have a call into the doctor who is on the prescription label. We are working on a subpoena." He turned when the door opened.

"Sir, you've got a call from Corbin's wife," he said. "And we also just got this over the fax." The officer handed Hank a piece of paper. I recognized the stamp at the top of the page. It was from the coroner's office.

"Okay. We are done here." Hank turned back to me.

"Is that the initial autopsy report?" I asked.

Hank paused, as though he were studying on whether to tell me or not.

"Yeah. Time of death is around eleven a.m." He gnawed on the inside of his jaw. "Corbin died of anaphylactic shock. Seems the inhaler might be his."

"Peanuts," I gasped.

"How did you know?" Hank's brows hooded over his eyes.

"Yesterday at the campground party, he was offered a peanut butter cookie. He refused it because he said he was allergic to peanuts. So why would he eat peanut butter?" There was something wrong with this picture.

"Let's get together in the morning over coffee to discuss all this and I'll let you know what I'd like you to listen out for because I agree with you. Something doesn't seem right." He rocked back on his heels.

"Okay." I nodded. "Since Jamison is in the bungalow alone, Penelope can stay with him."

"How is Fifi?" Hank asked.

"She's about to bust." I laughed.

"Granny Agnes wants a puppy." He smirked. "I'm sorry about what she said earlier. She's always sticking her nose in places it doesn't belong."

"Ah, it's okay." I brushed it off. "The family always likes me, it's the men that don't." I clamped my mouth shut, shocked I'd even said that.

"I'm sure you have no problem with men, Mae West." His face softened and his eyes lingered on my face.

"Sir?" The officer stuck his head back into the door.

"I'll see you in the morning." Hank brushed past me and out the door. His cologne brushed past my nose, filling my lungs and teasing my heart.

When I left the room where Hank had questioned me, I found Penelope sitting next to Jamison, waiting for her turn in the interrogation room. Jamison told me he'd wait for Penelope and bring her back to the campground since they weren't allowed to leave town, which made this a perfect time for me to question Alison Gilbert alone.

Her office was located in the Daniel Boone National Park office in the neighboring town. Since the police station was on the outskirts of town, it was close to her office and a quick ride.

The building was a typical brown brick building built in the sixties. The parking lot had only one car in it and it belonged to Alison. The last two windows on the side of the building were illuminated and I remembered those were the windows in the conference room where she'd interviewed me.

The front door was unlocked but the sign posted the hours. According to the time, the building should have been closed.

"Alison?" I hollered as I entered the building. There was

a deserted welcome desk with all the literature you'd ever need about the Daniel Boone National Park and surrounding towns. "It's me, Mae West."

My eyes scanned down the brochure holder and a smile crossed my face after I'd seen the new brochures for Happy Trails Campground that Abby Fawn had put together. They were gorgeous with the photos of the lake, recreation center, bungalows, and few campers. The families in the photos sure were having a good time. I remember when Abby and Alison had come to the campground to take those pictures. Abby had hired Alison to do them for us. It was a pretty reasonable fee too.

"Alison?" I called down the hall where I'd seen the lights coming out of the conference room. I headed on down the hallway. The place was big. She was probably going to the bathroom and would be back shortly.

The other office doors were shut. There were two skinny and long windows on each side of the doors, showing the darkness inside. It was deeply silent and eerie. The quiet had engulfed me with each step and I was a bit relieved when I made it to the light of the conference room. Until I stepped inside.

"Alison!" I screamed and ran over when I saw her lying on the floor with her arms in football goal position and her legs bent to one side. "Oh my God, oh my God," I panted as I took her into my arms and blood rushed out the back of her head.

I put her back down and rubbed my temples. My heart raced as I started to panic. I flailed my hands at my wrist as I paced back and forth, trying to gather my wits.

"Hank!" With trembling hands, somehow, I dialed Hank's number. "Hank, Alison is dead."

"What?" He gasped from the other end of the phone.

"Alison Gilbert is dead. Just come to the Daniel Boone National Park office," I told him to hurry up in a shaky voice.

There was no way I was staying inside with Alison. I ran outside to sit down on the curb in front of the building and wait for Hank.

CHAPTER 8

Not that I had a lot of time to wait until Hank and the slew of police cars pulled up, but to my brain, it felt like a long time to sit there on the curb and think about the dead woman in the building behind me. A woman with a secret.

"She said she had uncovered some things that Corbin didn't like. What were those things?" I asked myself and sat on my hands to keep them from trembling out of my skin. "Who else would know?"

The lights of a car blinded me like a spotlight, followed by the swirling blue and red lights of the cruisers.

"Mae, are you okay?" Hank jumped out of the first car and rushed over to me. There was a sincere look of concern on his face. He sat down next to me and peeled off his suit coat and draped it over my shoulders. The other officers ran past us with their guns drawn. Hank must've seen the look on my face. "They are going to clear the scene."

"You mean?" I jerked back and looked at him. "You think the killer is still in there." I gulped. "I didn't even think of that. I just ran out here."

"We don't know if there is a killer." He smiled.

"Huh? She was shot. In the head. I picked her up." It was then that I realized I probably shouldn't have picked her up in case it was a murder scene.

Hank looked at my shirt and I looked down. Alison's blood smeared all over it.

"We need to make sure it wasn't a self-inflicted gunshot." Did he think she killed herself? He continued, "I made it clear that she was a suspect in Corbin's case. Maybe she realized she was caught and her only way out was to kill herself."

"No. No." I shook my head. "She knew I was coming over here to meet with her."

"You were?" His expression grew still and serious. "You didn't mention that at the police station."

The coroner's white van pulled up along the curb to the left of us.

"I wanted to hear what she had to say." There wasn't any need to explain it to him since I'd not gotten the chance to ask her all the things I was keeping from him.

"What else are you keeping a secret in there?" He reached up and tapped his finger to my head.

"She uses an inhaler." I stood up to avoid looking at his reaction.

"Geez, Mae." There was an edge of anger in his voice. "You mean to tell me that you knew she used an inhaler and didn't say anything after I told you we found one at the scene?"

"I . . ." I searched for the words, but nothing seemed to come to mind

"You nothing. This could've been avoided if you'd told me that because she'd be in custody right now answering even more questions until the DNA results from the inhaler came back." He had stood up by the time I turned around to face him.

"Sir," the officer came out of the building. "It's all clear. The deceased is down the hall and in the last conference room on the right."

Hank glowered at me and turned away to go into the building.

There were so many unanswered questions that I needed to answer. What did Corbin know so he had to threaten Alison? What did Alison have in that file? Where was the file?

Hank was wrong. Alison didn't kill herself. Someone knew what information Corbin and Alison had and killed both of them to keep them quiet. Someone wanted them to stay silent and there was no surer way to silence them than killing them.

Another set of car lights brought me out of my head. Queenie French and Abby Fawn jumped out of the car.

"There she is!" Abby yelled and the two ran over to me. "What's going on?"

My brows knitted and my jaw dropped as I looked between them.

"Police scanner," was all Queenie had to say.

"Come on," Abby encouraged me to walk forward from where my shoes felt like they were filled with concrete. "Let's get you back to The Laundry Club. All the girls are there."

"Yeah. We called them on the way over here to get over there and put on a pot of pumpkin spice coffee," Queenie said.

Pumpkin spice was my favorite. Especially this time of the year and it would for sure make me feel a tiny bit better.

This situation was like Christmas for these ladies. They

couldn't wait until they got the scoop.

"She's in shock." Abby put her face in mine.

I wasn't sure if I was in shock or I was just so happy they were there and I wasn't alone.

"You drive Mae's car back and I'll drive her back." Abby tucked her fingers in my front pocket where my keys to the Ford Escort were and she tossed them to Queenie.

Queenie did some sort of Jazzercise grapevine dance move and caught them in her hand on the last back foot cross move.

I laughed.

"All the moves come in handy." Queenie wiggled her brows and grapevined back the other way on the way towards my car.

"Yeah. She said she needed to get her steps in and was on her way to a Jazzercise class when the scanner picked up the news about Alison." Abby guided me towards the car.

"The coat. Hank." My mouth was dry.

"You keep that coat on. This fall weather is crazy and it's cold out here tonight." She wrapped her arms around my shoulder and patted them. She opened the passenger door of her car and helped me in.

The cool breeze swept in when she shut the door, sending a chill up my legs and leaving my arms with goose-bumps. I curled the lapels of the suit coat around me and looked out the window. The moon was high in the sky, even though it was only about seven p.m. Some of the tree branches looked like spikes without their freshly fallen leaves, while some of them were still full and vibrant with color. The faint smell of Hank was imbedded in the fibers of his coat and somehow it make me feel safe. I snuggled it a little closer, warding off the goosebumps all over my body.

It was the strange time of the year when it was cool in

the morning. When you left the house, you'd need to carry a light jacket or sweatshirt. In the afternoon, the sun was out and heated up the world around us, making us peel off that outer layer, only for the cold to return once the sun set. It was a cruel joke Mother Nature played on Kentucky, but I enjoyed every season. Especially the fall.

Abby got into the car and she assured me that everything was going to be okay, but I wasn't sure of it. Especially since she'd yet to hear what I had to say.

While she drove, she must've known I needed the space and silence. She did look over a few times at my shirt where Alison's blood was smeared. I continued to look forward, still gathering and processing what had happened since I'd talked to Alison in the police station parking lot.

My mind was like a hamster wheel. The same images of me holding Alison played over and over, almost making feel as if I were going nuts. No matter how hard I tried, I couldn't get off the wheel of the image.

"Mae," Abby said my name and gently touched my arm. "We're here. Do you want me to take you home instead?"

"No," I whispered. "I need to be with my friends. But Fifi."

"Dottie said she'd get Fifi and bring her here." Abby always thought of everything. "You're shaking. Let's get you inside and out of that shirt. Get you into something warm."

I did what she told me to do and got out of the car. I let her guide me inside of the Laundry Club where the smell of the freshly brewed coffee from the coffee bar perked me right up.

"Mae, what on earth is that?" Dottie's nose curled. "Is that blood?" she shrieked.

"Oh, Mae." Betts Hager rushed over, setting down the cup of coffee on the card table just inside of the door. The cup was probably meant for me, but not to enjoy with a bloody shirt.

"Move it." Queenie pushed through the door and past us.

"Queenie, don't be so rude," Betts scolded her. "She's been through a lot over the past couple of days. Haven't you any compassion."

Since Betts was the preacher's wife, she always tried to be kind and use nice words around this group of women who let anything and everything come out of their mouth.

"What are you doing?" Betts rushed over to Queenie, who was doing a great job at ignoring her. "That's not your laundry."

Queenie jerked open the door of one of the dryers and dumped the clothes into one of the rolling baskets.

"Nope, but it's been sitting in this dryer all day long." She pulled up different pieces of clothing before she settled on a long-sleeved shirt with the state of Texas printed on the front. "If they are going to leave it here and not come back, then they deserve to have it used for the greater good."

"And what is the greater good?" Betts wanted to know and she had the right to know. After all, she did own The Laundry Club and she would have to explain to the customer why they were missing their favorite Texas shirt, if it were their favorite.

"Look at Mae." Queenie shoved past Betts. "If this isn't for the greater good, then I'm not sure what is."

Betts looked me up and down.

"Is that...?" she asked me and pointed.

"Blood. Alison Gilbert's blood from the gunshot to her head. The back of her head." I suddenly snapped out of the shock. "She didn't kill herself." I looked at each one of my friends. "She was killed. If she shot herself in the head, her head would be half missing. I mean, it's what it shows in the movies. But her face." The images of her perfectly put together face joined the hamster wheel image of her lifeless body. "Someone shot her from afar and it came out the back of her head or neck." I blinked, not fully knowing where the blood had come from, but according to the images in my head of my holding her, I'd held her head up to my shirt.

"Okay, let's get this off and get you warmed up." Queenie peeled off Hank's suit coat from my shoulders. "Is this Detective Hank's?" There was a change in her tone that was excited. "Mmmhhhh," she brought the coat up to her nose, "it's his smell alright. Delish."

"Stop that." Abby jerked the jacket from her. "Just change her shirt."

The two of them worked on getting me out of my shirt. Queenie handed it off to Abby, who rushed over to one of the washing machines to wash it. Queenie tugged the customer's shirt she stole out of the dryer over my head and on instinct, I pushed my arms into the sleeves.

Queenie guided me over to the area where we had our book club, near the bookshelf filled with books to be read by the customers who came in to do their laundry.

"Wait." I stopped and looked around. The walls of the laundry room had been painted a nice red and the chairs had been upgraded from metal chairs to a few large, cotton red ones that accented the wall color and a couple of new leather couches. A new coffee table positioned in front of the television. "When did you redo all of this?"

"We have been helping out a few young people who had to do some community service. The furniture was delivered this morning." Betts patted for me to sit in one of the chairs and they took their places around me. "Lester has a soft spot and thinks he can just rehab all of them."

"That's nice." Even though the tension about what happened to Alison earlier was hanging in the air, it was nice to think about something different and kind for even just a second.

"Yeah, well, one of the ones we truly thought was going to go out and do great things after he was released from jail did really good the other day when we went into the park and picked up trash." Betts sighed.

"Can you believe people just throw their trash all over like that?" Abby growled.

"What about the kid?" I asked getting back to Betts's story, because if we weren't careful, we would trail off in a completely different direction.

"We went back yesterday morning to finish up and after a couple of hours of collecting trash, he just darted off. Lester ran after him, but this kid was fast," Betts said.

Dottie Swaggert walked into the laundromat and let Fifi down after my sweet pup noticed me. Fifi's belly swayed back and forth as she waddled over to me. I bent down and picked her up, placing her and her belly full of babies in my lap. She looked up with those pitiful, help me get these out of me eyes. I gave her kissy lips and she licked me.

"You mean to tell me he escaped?" Queenie's head jerked up and she had a scowl on her face. "These youngins', I just don't get them."

"Me neither." Dottie groaned, as she caught the tail end of the conversation. "Yesterday this kid was hiking and ran off the Red Fox Trail like some sort of crazy kid. He was hooting and hollering. It look like the devil himself got into that kid. He's probably on some sort of drugs."

"Stop." I pointed to Dottie and then looked at Betts. "You said this was yesterday morning?"

"Yes. Why?" She became instantly wide awake. "No," she

gasped and threw her hand over her mouth. "You don't think he had anything to do with. . ." her voice trailed off. "We were near the campground." She blinked back the same thoughts I was having.

"Were you all in the same area picking up trash?" I asked her. I had a nigglin' suspicion this kid knew something or saw something. Or was he the killer?

"Stop right there." Abby jumped up and ran over to the Laundry Club office, emerging with a pad of paper and a pen. "I think we need to write this all down. Kinda like what Mae did when Tammy Jo was the suspect in the murder of Fifi's nanny."

She made a good point. I did write everything down, from suspect to motive, and it seemed to help sort out the puzzles pieces. We continued to talk while Abby scribbled down notes.

"We were spread out on the trail. We parked in the parking lot of the public picnic area where the Red Fox Trail starts on Park Drive. We were instructed to stay on that trail since it is one of the most popular for tourists to see all the color changes of the season."

Red Fox Trail had every part of autumn. There was a nice creek that bubbled over the rocks with a soothing sound, where I wanted to end up with Ty that day. The sun rose and set perfectly over the trail as the days grew shorter. The trees were the perfect colors of the season and hung down just enough to give light and shade.

"Lester had gone to the courthouse to see if there were any inmates that needed community service hours. The mayor said she'd gather some because she'd been on the Red Fox Trail earlier in the week and noticed a bunch of trash." Betts shrugged.

"What time did he run?" I weeded out through the other

parts of her story to get to the point.

"It was around eleven when Lester started rounding all the inmates up." She lifted her chin, she waved her hand. "I mean, this is a long shot. We told the police immediately and they said they'd send someone."

My mouth dried. Hank had said the coroner's initial report noted Corbin's time of death was around eleven a.m. Ty and I weren't there until after 1 p.m.

"Do you think they sent Corbin to find him?" Abby asked a great question.

"Nope," Dottie chimed in. "I'd called the park ranger's office because we have a camper missing."

"I'm sending out an alert." Abby began to put out on social media about a lost camper. "It's no different than an Amber Alert."

"Corbin went on the trail to look for our camper and it was the last time I'd seen him." Dottie finished her story.

"Dottie," I said and turned towards her. "Do you remember what this person looked like that ran out of the woods?"

"You know I wasn't paying attention to what they looked like. I was paying attention to the flailing and carryin' on like a crazy person on drugs," she said.

"You can't remember nothing?" I gave her the "come on" look. "It could be important."

"I know they are criminals, but they are white-collar criminals," Betts reminded me of the offenses that had landed them into the county jail. "They stole things from Deters, or they skipped paying for gas at Grassel's. Not killed anyone."

"Did you offer any sort of food with peanuts in it?" I asked.

"We always offer some food that's prepared by the Bible

Thumpers," she referred to the women in the church that made food for everything. "But yesterday, we did stop by the Cookie Crumble and let them pick out the cookies they wanted."

"Oh, no," I groaned. "The coroner's initial report said Corbin's time of death was around 11 a.m. and he died of anaphylactic shock due to his peanut allergy."

"He did say he was allergic to peanuts when I offered him a peanut butter cookie at the campground party," Betts recalled.

"Maybe Corbin's death was an accident." Queenie pointed out.

"How so?" Abby questioned.

"What if Corbin was on the trail looking for this crazy kid after Lester had called the police. When Corbin found him on the trail, maybe the kid offered him one of his cookies and dropped dead. The kid freaked out and ran, figuring he'd be in trouble for the death of Corbin." That was probably the smartest thing I'd ever heard Queenie say.

"That sounds all fine and dandy, but it doesn't explain Alison Gilbert," Abby played the devil's advocate.

"She may have killed herself, though I don't think she did. When I was there, her death hadn't been ruled a homicide yet," I wanted to make it very clear. "She could've thought he was killed over her article."

It was a long stretch, but I was hoping for anything that would tell my soul there wasn't a killer on the loose.

My phone chirped a text. It was from Hank.

"Mae?" Dottie said my name, but it was like I was in a fog. "Are you okay? Your face is as white as a sheet."

My eyes slid up and gazed at her. Sheer panic swept through me.

My soul was right.

CHAPTER 9

H ank's text, I'd gotten at the Laundry Club, confirmed Alison was murdered. The trajectory of the bullet had actually come from outside the window. Alison didn't see it coming. My only hope was that she felt no pain and died fast.

"Coward," I whispered in anger as I thought of how cowardly the killer was.

After the news had come, the girls and I had made a laundry list - no pun intended - of suspects. There was one person not on the list that I'd kept to myself. We'd decided at the end of the night that we'd keep our eyes and ears open and report back on anything out of the ordinary.

I reached over and rubbed the pad of paper Abby had been writing on. I took it home with me because I knew I wanted to go over it over and over again. I dragged it across the small kitchen table in my camper and started to read through it after I'd gotten Fifi settled down for the night. Or at least I'd thought I'd gotten her settled down for the night.

The knock at the door startled me and took me out of my train of thought.

"Mae, are you home?" Ty asked from the other side of the door.

"Just a minute," I hollered back and took a quick glance at my reflection in the microwave door.

Listen, space was limited in a camper and I had to do with what I had. The black door on the microwave was going to have to be my mirror. My curly hair was now a bush around my head, springing up all over the place. I wrapped my hands around it like I was putting it in a ponytail to see if the sweat from my hands would tame it, but it sprung right back out after I let go.

The metal door of the camper swung out wide. He caught it before it swung back and slammed shut. He put one foot up on the step.

"Hey, there." I took a step back to make some room. "Come on in."

"I brought beer." He lifted up a six pack of brew. "I heard about Alison and figured you could use something to help you sleep."

He stepped up in to my camper. My skin prickled pleasurably as his arm brushed up against mine on the way in.

"Hey, girl," Ty's voice quickly changed into his Fifi voice. She was no longer settled as she shook her tail. "You are about to bust." There was some empathy in his voice. "How much longer?" He glanced behind his shoulder at me with sad eyes.

"Soon." I'd not really kept an exact count, though I could go back and count the days since it was at the summer solstice party where Roscoe, the pug, put her under his spell. "I guess I could call the doctor and have her check Fifi out."

"I'm sure she's fine. If there's not been any problems, I

guess nature will take its course." He gave her another couple of good scratches and then stood back up.

He slipped two beers from the six-pack sleeve. He twisted the top off before he handed me mine. It was that whole southern gentleman thing that made me melt. If this was Hank, I'd had to twist off my own top.

"What on earth are you working on here?" He took a drink of his beer and looked down at the pad of paper. "Mayor MacKenzie?" He looked at me.

"Here are the things I know." I pointed to the diagram Abby had started and I was working on. "There was an inmate missing from his community service duties at the same time Corbin had eaten the cookie."

"Inmate? Cookie?" He'd obviously not heard all the gossip.

I quickly explained to him the initial autopsy report of Corbin's cause of death and how Lester had taken a few of the local inmates to do some of their community service hours on the Red Fox Trail at the time of Corbin's death. I also told him how the bus with the inmates stopped by the Cookie Crumble.

"What doesn't make sense is why did Corbin eat the cookie? Did the inmate have a peanut butter cookie? The first answer that would lead me to the rest of these answers were going to come from Christine Watson at the Cookie Crumble." I clicked the pen to expose the tip and circled Christine's name a few times.

"Do you think she's going to remember what they ordered?" He asked.

"She will remember what cookies she'd baked. I'd asked her how she decided what cookies to display and she said that she only baked a couple different types of cookies a day. She'll know what cookies and possibly how many were gone or maybe who bought what." It was a long shot worth checking out.

"Do you know what the inmate looks like? Or his name?" Ty was good at playing devil's advocate, which made me only want to figure this out more.

"No, but I do know that I can get on Jailtracker.com and see if I can pull him up." I made a quick note next to the inmate's motive, which I wrote down as wanting to escape and Corbin tried to stop him and added a trip to the library to do some research on Abby's work computer. Maybe after my hair appointment.

"That's a great idea, if you knew his name." Ty dragged the bottle up to his lips and took a drink. "Do you think Alison's murder is related?"

"Well, if Corbin's death was accidental and he did eat the cookie, my thought about the inmate was that he happened upon the body and took off because he didn't want anyone to think he'd killed him, which makes his death not related to Alison." I continued to point the tip of the pen back and forth between the two.

"You've done a lot of thinking on this." Ty smiled.

"I talked to Alison outside of the police station. She said that she'd found out some information and Corbin had threatened her. Something about if she continued to snoop into the drought thing and ran an article, he'd get the paper shut down. How could he do that?" I asked and thought that was a good question to research so I wrote that down next to Alison's name. "Which makes me think," I tapped my temple, "whoever killed Alison knew she had some information and wanted to keep her silent, tying the two deaths together."

"Really we only know of one murder. Alison." There he went again with common sense and true facts.

"Yes." I took a drink of the beer and continued to ponder the list of suspects in front of me.

"Alison had a file with a bunch of information in it."

"I guess you want that file." He inhaled sharply.

"I do." I wondered if Hank had it.

"Don't forget William Hinson is missing and he had the major confrontation with Corbin the day before Corbin's death, found out his fiancée was having an affair with his best friend right before their wedding, and he went missing around the time Corbin's death occurred. This might be a long shot, but I'd think William would be Hank's number one suspect in at least Corbin's murder." I talked so fast, Ty was blinking rapidly trying to keep up.

"That's a mouthful." He took another deep breath. "How is the mayor fitting into all this?" He circled his beer around the top of the paper.

"Lester got the idea to have the inmates clean the trail from the Mayor. I wonder if she had something to do with Corbin dragging his feet on the shutdown of the park due to the drought. He certainly couldn't shut it down if he was dead."

"Dragging his feet?" Ty asked.

"Yeah, it was something Alison said to me. She said that Corbin had been dragging his feet and she had this list of shutdowns Corbin had done. It included the time between when the drought threat to the park was determined to the shutdown. There were only hours between them, but not this drought. There's been several weeks that've gone by since he first reported shutting down because of the drought." I looked back down at the list.

Nothing on there made any sort of complete puzzle or sense, for that matter. It was just a bunch of words and suspicion.

"You're really going to help Hank?" Ty sat down on the small leather couch and rested his ankle on his knee.

"I would like to help find out where William is. He is my camper and it truly doesn't look good that he's disappeared." The lights coming down the campground road got my attention. I leaned over the sink and noticed it was Jamison's car. I watched him and Penelope get out of the car. The dark starry night was giving off just enough light for me to see their silhouettes making their way towards the bungalow. "Anyways, I can dig around a bit to see what I can find out."

"Do you think we need to talk about what happened on the trail?" He asked.

"I thought we'd just spent the last ten minutes talking about it." I eased down on the couch next to him. My knees pointing towards him.

"I'm talking about what happened between me and you." He gestured his beer between us. "It seems like every time we go to do something or get closer, we are tugged apart. Plus the fact that you told Hank you were going back to work instead of meeting me after you got my text."

"I'm sorry I didn't tell Hank. But I didn't think he needed to know. I didn't lie to you. I did go to the bank and when I saw the newspaper article Alison had written, I got mad. Then I saw her near the amphitheater and I took off after her." It was best to tell Ty the entire truth. "That's when I saw Hank."

He nodded his head and stared at me.

"That's your answer, huh?" He questioned.

I wasn't sure what he wanted me to say.

"It's the truth." Was I wrong and he didn't want the truth?

"I do agree that something always comes up or between

us when we've tried to get together." His face drew a blank once my words seemed to sink in.

He stood up.

"I've got to go. It's getting late and I've got to get up early." He took one last swig of his beer and threw it away in the trashcan underneath my sink. "You can keep the beers."

His attitude had completely changed. The sensitive side of him had turned into a cold shoulder for me, but not Fifi. He rubbed her a few times and said his goodbyes to her before he turned to look at me.

"We'll talk later." He gave the head nod before he opened the door. "Try and get some sleep. Don't let anyone know you're snooping around. Lock the door when I leave."

I forced a smile and wished somehow, I'd given him an answer that would satisfy him. I had hurt Ty and he was the last person I wanted to hurt.

The night left me and Fifi restless. Fifi couldn't get comfortable no matter how many times she tried to lay down. My mind couldn't slow down to give me a restful sleep.

I wanted it to be Ty that kept me up, but it was the notepad with all my ideas of what happened to Corbin and Alison that swirled around in my head.

Instead of trying to fight it any longer, I decided to get up and plan out my day.

I'd gotten Fifi out to go potty while I waited for my coffee to brew. There still some time left until the coffee was ready, so I filled Fifi's bowl with some kibble and headed to the bathroom to get showered. I had enough time to head over to the police station and see Agnes before I went to my hair appointment at Cute-icles at noon.

"Are you not hungry?" I noticed Fifi hadn't touched her

food. I bent down and picked her up. She stiffened up when I felt her belly. "Are you about to have your babies?"

I put her in her little bed. She seemed the most comfortable there, though that wasn't saying much. I would have Dottie check on her throughout the morning and afternoon while I was gone. Before I forgot, I texted Dottie knowing she wasn't awake yet, but she'd get it once she got up.

The sound of tires driving through the campground made me look out the window.

"Hank," I gasped and forgotten I'd agreed to him stopping by.

Once again, I tried to get a look at my reflection. Wet hair and all, but at least my skinny jeans and tight pink sweater looked cute with my silver flip flops. Not that I was trying to impress him. I grabbed his coat that he'd let me use off the chair. I might've taken one more sniff, but I'd never tell.

I opened the door and walked out under my camper's retractable canopy, waving to him as he pulled up. From the opposite direction another car was coming.

It made my heart stop when Ty drove by, slowly, staring at me as I greeted Hank with a big smile. My smile faltered and I waved at Ty, only he zoomed off. Just another incident where I was going to have to explain myself.

"Good morning," I greeted Hank and held out his coat.

"He didn't like seeing me here this early," Hank snickered, his eyes drawing up and down my body. He took the coat and threw it in his car before he slammed the door shut and walked up to the camper. "Maybe he thinks you were telling me goodbye from a passionate night." He winked. His green eyes popped against his ivory skin and black hair. Today he didn't have on his usual suit. He had on a pair of jeans and a long-sleeved button-down shirt.

"Shut up." I rolled my eyes and sighed. This was exactly why I called Ty a southern gentleman and Hank a little gruffer. Ty would've said good morning where Hank just bypassed it completely.

"Come on in. You're just in time for coffee." The strong scent of pumpkin spice floated out the door and circled around my nose.

Hank followed me in. Just like Ty, he immediately went to talk to Fifi. While Fifi charmed him like she did Ty, I took out a couple mugs and poured us some coffee.

"I could smell the coffee outside." He did at least smile. He stood up.

"I think she's about to have the babies." I handed him his cup. "She tightened up when I felt her belly."

"How's her appetite?" He asked and took that first sip. I could see he enjoyed it. His stern jaw melted and his shoulders relaxed.

"Funny you should ask." I leaned up against the counter facing him. "Last night she ate all her food. She was restless all night. She wasn't hungry this morning."

"It's a sign." His eyes darted between me and Fifi overtop the mug. "When they feel full and uncomfortable, it's usually going to come soon."

Fifi looked up with her pitiful round and black eyes like she knew we were talking about her.

He dragged the paper I'd been pondering over last night closer to him.

"It looks like you've been doing a lot of theories on this paper." He continued to look at it. "Yesterday I told you I'd be by to discuss what I would like you to look into since everyone seems to tell you things and I'd figured it was best to join forces with you instead of working against you."

I couldn't help but smile.

"As you can see, there are several different suspects other than Penelope and Jamison, though I do think they are still contenders." I shrugged and took another drink.

"That's why I'm here." He sat back in the chair. "There's no evidence Corbin was murdered. This looks like two separate crimes."

"What about the inmate?" I asked.

"Stanley Bayer," Hank said the inmates name. "He is still at large. He was probably just trying to escape and he does have a history of mania. It appears he was worked up in his head when he saw Lester and then Dottie."

"You're telling me that you think he accidentally ate peanut butter?" I asked, thinking it was strange that a man of Corbin's age all of the sudden slipped up and ate something with peanut butter.

"It appears so." He tapped the pad. "So thanks, but we don't need you to look into anything."

"What about Alison?" I crossed my arms over my chest. "She was murdered and it had to do with the drought which has to do with Corbin."

"We are looking at all angles." He took another drink and stood up. "Alison had her nose into a lot of things, not just the drought."

"Like what?" I asked smugly.

"Don't make me regret asking you to help out with Corbin." He gave me a blank look. "Anyways, thank you for the coffee. I've got to get out of here."

I stewed as I watched him get up. I'd spent the better part of my life yesterday trying to figure out who killed Corbin and Alison. Even if it was separate incidents, which I'd said yesterday was a possibility.

Hank opened the door. The sunrise was midway up in the sky. Clouds of yellow and orange drifted just above the mountain tree line over the Daniel Boone National Park painted a beautiful picture.

"Gosh. That's amazing." Hank's sensitive side, that was rarely seen, had made an appearance. He continued to look at the sunrise and walked down the two steps.

I wasn't going to let him get away with firing me so easy.

"You could've just texted me that you didn't need me anymore." I grabbed the handle of the metal door, my arm extended.

"Maybe I wanted to see you." He winked.

CHAPTER 10

"He winked?" Abby Fawn leaned over the desk, propped up on her elbows while she watched me type Stanley Bayer's name on the Jailtracker.com website.

The Normal County Public Library was quiet this time of the morning. It was the perfect time to get on the computers before the elderly in the community came in and played their games or looked up all their medications, which was a common occurrence since most of them didn't have computers at their homes. I'd thought about getting a laptop and hadn't. It wasn't a priority in my life and social media wasn't something I did like Abby did. It was much nicer just to pay her to do all the social media marketing for Happy Trails.

"Mmhhh," I ho-hummed and dragged my eyes down the screen at the alphabetical names. There were only a few inmates in the jail. After I found his name, I clicked on it and his rap sheet pulled up.

"I've lived here all my life and I've never had one guy fall over me, much less two." She pushed up and leaned her hip on the desk, using her finger to twirl the end of her ponytail. "Oh, well." She leaned back down. "So this is the guy that's escaped?"

We both stared at his mugshot. He didn't look like a maniac, as Hank has said was in his record. He had short, light brown hair cut above his ears. His sideburns were a little longer than a normal side burn but I'd noticed in the magazines in line at Grassel's Gas Station that the men had been wearing them longer. Or maybe it was because Stanley, here, was incarcerated and didn't have access to a good razor. Either way, none of the list of his charges said he'd killed someone, stolen anything, or really committed any crime other than getting a few DUI while hiking. This time it looks like he was in for a thirty day stay.

"Hashtag criminal on the loose. Hashtag where is Stanley Bayer. Hashtag Stanley Bayer where are you." Abby texted away on her social media account.

"Abby, stop." I gave her a cross look. "We are trying to grow the economy, not scare people off."

"Oh." Her fingers started tapping so fast. "There. Delete." She looked up, gave a hard nod, and smiled. "Hashtag Happy Trails Campground, hashtag fall family fun, hashtag amazing sunrises, hashtag romance and winking men."

"Stop it." My jaw dropped. I knew she was referring to what'd happened with Hank. I ignored her while she gushed on about how romantic it really was that he'd come over right before sunrise and timed it perfect to see it come up over the horizon. I hit the print icon so I could keep Stanley Bayer's face in front of me.

I didn't care what Hank Sharp thought. I knew my gut and my gut told me something wasn't right. I couldn't shake the notion that Stanley could've seen something. If I could find Stanley and ask him a few questions, then I'd feel better.

"I thought you said Hank believes these are two separate cases?" Abby picked up the stack of books she'd laid on the desk when she noticed I was there.

"That's what he said." I reached underneath the desk where the piece of paper popped up with Stanley's mugshot printed on it along with his rap sheet.

In the search engine, I typed in Stanley's name and White Pages. It gave me a listing for a person with his name that lived in Normal. I quickly wrote down the address on the sheet I'd just printed. I'd do a drive-by and check it out.

More than likely the detective's office or even the police have gone there if it was his house to make sure he'd not gone there after the escape. He'd be pretty stupid to, but it was the only thing I had at this moment.

"What are you two doing?" Queenie popped her head around the non-fiction travel section bookshelf.

"I'm going to put these books back and Miss Private Eye is going to go spy on someone's house." Abby took off in the opposite direction with the books stacked in her arms. She did a few steps to the left and then to the right as she tried to balance them on her way.

"Oh, investigation." Queenie vigorously rubbed her hands together before she tucked her thumbs in the elastic of her black leggings. She had on a teal zipper jacket and her fanny pack clipped around her waist. "Queenie is at your service." She shook one hand into jazz hands in the air while the other hand held a romance paperback. She stuck the toe of her bright white tennis shoe out. "I love me a good investigation."

"You don't have class?" I asked wondering why she

wasn't in the basement of the Normal Baptist Church teaching her morning class.

"Nope. The Bible Thumpers have something going on over there with Detective Hank Sharp, so they made me cancel. So I've got all morning to hang out with you since everyone else from the Laundry Club is working." She shimmied her shoulders at the same time she bent her knees and did a couple of squats. More Jazzercise moves.

"Your shoes are too white. They'll see us coming like a bright sun." I held my hand up to shield my eyes as a joke.

"I can help you." She picked up the paper with Stanley's photo. "I know Snookie Bayer. Her boy is Stanley. They live out on Welcome Home Road down yonder near the water plant."

"How well do you know Snookie Bayer?" I asked.

"Well enough that if I stopped by to visit, she'd not pull her shotgun out on me like she would on someone she didn't know." Queenie's lip twisted up on the corner. "You, she'd definitely cock the trigger."

"Did you say Hank was talking to the Bible Thumpers?" This was a bit of information that could help me.

"Yep. Why? What's on your mind?" She arched a sly brow.

"Before we go see Snookie Bayer, I'd like to make a stop and see Agnes Swift." I grabbed the paper and gathered all my belongings. "Down at the police station."

"What are you waiting for?" She did a quick two-step leading into a grapevine Jazzercise move. "I'm ready."

She did the grapevine move all the way to the front of the library. Abby laughed when she saw us leaving. I shook my head. What on earth had I gotten myself into?

"Why do you want to see Stanley?" Queenie asked from the passenger side.

"He escaped from his community service through Normal Baptist Church at the time of death of Corbin Ashbrook.

"Now, them Bayer boys are a handful and they've given Snookie a heck of a lot of trouble, but none of them boys would hurt a soul." Queenie always had the gossip. She'd lived here her entire sixty something years, since she'd never reveal her true age,

"I don't know. I'm going on a hunch he saw something that made him run out of the woods." It was only a guess. "He only had thirty days in the jail and he was halfway through according to Jail tracker."

"Snookie was pretty upset the first time Stanley came home wasted. She said she wasn't going to let any more of her boys suck the juice, but it's in their blood. Their daddy was a drunk and drunk himself to death. But Snookie, she was a nipper here and there." Queenie looked out the window, taking in the fall foliage. "It's gonna be a cold winter."

"Why do you say that?" I asked.

"I can feel it in my bones." She rubbed up and down her arms. She settled back into the seat and closed her eyes. A good indication she was done talking.

While she caught a quick nap on our short trip out to the police station, I turned my thoughts back to Alison. My main reason for seeing Agnes was to ask if she knew what Hank had found out about Alison's murder. Even though he had told me to stop snooping since they thought Corbin's death was accidental, that didn't make the fact that Alison was murdered any less painful. She was starting to confide in me and I wanted to know what she was going to say to me when we'd planned to meet.

I cracked the windows like Queenie was a dog I was

leaving in the car after I put the car in park and turned it off. There were some snorts and snores coming from her, so I left her there. I needed her at her best for when we went to see Snookie Bayer.

Agnes wasn't sitting at the sliding glass window when I opened the door to the police station, which meant I couldn't get rung into the police station.

I curled up on my toes and knocked on the glass with the middle knuckle on my pointer finger. It was enough to get an officer's attention. He shot a finger up in the air for me to hold on. In a few seconds, Agnes emerged from the hallway. When she noticed it was me, she put a big grin on her face.

She shooed me over to the door where she buzzed me in.

"Well? How was coffee?" There was an unexpected greeting on her face that told me she'd expected more than Hank firing me from snooping when I'd barely gotten started.

"Maybe I need to give you my phone number for you to warn me when he's stopping by to fire me." I snarled.

"Fired you?" There was an element of surprise on Agnes's face, that made her saggy eighty-year-old jowls drip down even more. She scratched her gray head of hair with her pointer finger. "That don't make sense." She pinched her lips. "He was prepared to…hmmm…fired you?"

"The other day he asked me to look into Corbin Ashbrook's death and this morning he said they believe Corbin might've died accidentally." I was laying the foundation to get some information out of her.

"Mae West, you aren't one to beat around the bush just because I'm an old lady, are you?" Agnes Swift was one smart cookie.

"I should've known." I leaned in closer so the officers over at the coffee pot couldn't hear. "I was wondering if they cleared the crime scene at the Daniel Boone National Park office where Alison Gilbert was killed."

"They finished it off this morning. Hank is working double time as the lead investigator in her murder and finishing up as a ranger in Corbin's death. He's not been too open about the Gilbert case. He said I would tell you and he's right." She nodded.

"Who is working on Stanley Bayer's escape?" I asked.

"Normal police. We've gotten some leads but they're not real. Some people called said they seen him in Florida. Then another call came in and said he was in Alaska." She rolled her eyes. "It was probably that mama of his."

"Snookie?" I asked.

"Mmhhh," she snorted. "Them boys give her a fit, but she loves that Stanley best of all."

"So I heard." I sighed. "Back to Alison's case. Are there any suspects?"

"Hank seems to think she was snooping around in something and apparently got a little too close. So they are going through her files on her computer. Technology these days, they think them computers hold all the answers to life." She tsked.

"I don't own one, but I do go to the library to use one," I said. "Alison told me Corbin had been dragging his feet on closing down the park for the drought. She also said he'd threatened her. Do you think Corbin was protecting someone?"

"Could've been." Agnes leaned in and mumbled, "According to his wife, Ardine, she said he got a phone call right before he left that morning. She said he was all hush-hush and told her he had to go look into something."

"Did you say Ardine?" I asked, repeating the name to make a mental note.

"Yep. She's just beside herself with grief. I told Hank to have the Bible Thumpers stop by there with an apple pie from Pam Purcell." Agnes licked her lips.

"You mean Carol Wise?" I asked.

"Nope. Carol has the best peaches in the summer, but Pam has the best apples in the fall." She corrected me.

I'd yet to meet Carol or Pam, though I knew all about their pie baking feud.

"Do you think an apple turnover from the Cookie Crumble will do?" I asked.

"If it's coming from you, anything will be fine." Agnes patted me on the back. "Be sure to let me know what you find out, because Hank has been tightlipped. And before you go digging to come up with something about Corbin, you're wasting your time. The autopsy report came back one-hundred percent that Corbin died of anaphylaxis. His body shows all the signs."

She handed me the final report from the coroner. I read the notes around the body outline on the paper about Corbin's swollen eyes, the rash on his body, and how his tongue was the weapon that killed him. Closed off his airway. It did appear that Hank was right. They were two separate incidents. It didn't change my mind about going to see Ardine. Not only did I want to give my condolences, I wanted to see if she knew anything about what Alison had said about Corbin and if she knew how he really felt about the drought. After all, they were husband and wife, you'd figure they'd told each other everything.

"Why did you think Hank was coming over this morning?" I had to ask. I was so curious.

"Mae West, have you ever heard of island time?" She

asked. "Slow life but the most enjoyable while you're there?" she asked, and I nodded.

"Nothing like it." I recalled the time Paul had taken me to the western Caribbean and it was the most relaxing vacation I'd ever been on.

"Well, honey, you're on Hank Sharp time." She winked and answered the ringing phone.

"Hank Sharp time," I whispered on my way out.

Was he really worth the wait?

CHAPTER 11

"Why are we back here?" Sleeping Beauty, aka Queenie French, popped up from her slumber in the passenger seat after I'd pulled into a parking space in front of the Cookie Crumble.

There was a white work van in front of the bakery with the logo of a security company on it. There was a man standing on a ladder, screwing something on front of the building.

"While you were sleeping..." I started to say.

"I was resting my eyes," she debated.

"You were snoring." The facts were the facts.

"Why are we here?" She ignored me and pulled herself together.

"I need to get something with apple in it from Christine and I have a few questions for her too." I looked past Queenie and into the window of the bakery.

There were a couple of customers at the counter. For a split second, I debated whether or not to wait until they left. Then again, if I went in, Christine might hurry them along. I decided to do the latter.

The bell of the door dinged. Christine looked up from the glass display case. The freckles sprinkled spread across her face as her smile grew. Her hair was tucked under the normal hair net.

"Good morning," she trilled through the shop. Her upbeat demeanor was welcomed. "I'll be right with you two."

Queenie trotted up to the counter and joined the other two customers. She started to give her two cents on her favorite desserts Christine had baked for the day.

"While she makes me a sale, what can I get for you?" Christine walked over. She smelled like a warm glazed donut.

"I need to get something with apple in it for Corbin Ashbrook's wife." I threw it in so I could dive into the questioning about the cookies and pastries she'd sold the inmates when Betts had brought them here before they went to pick up trash.

"Such a tragedy." A frown flitted across her face. "I'd heard it was from eating peanut butter, which is really odd because he came in here every Friday and would hunt for something without peanut butter." She drew her hand to her chest. "I can't make this a peanut-free facility. But on Fridays, when I'd get here early, I'd make one batch of sugar cookies before I did anything with other cookies because there was no trace of peanuts that early."

"That is so nice of you." I didn't expect any different. Christine was a very nice person and had always been so considerate of others.

"He didn't come today." She glanced over at the counter behind her. "That's his cookie and he didn't come get it."

This wasn't adding up to a death by peanut allergy. Why

hadn't he stopped by the bakery? These were all questions maybe Ardine could answer.

"Are you having a security system installed?" I asked. Normal really never had true crime like robberies or break-ins. Maybe a couple of murders, but those weren't because the crime rate was through the roof. In fact, Normal had very little crime.

"I'd heard there was someone lingering around the window last night. It kinda scared me since the park does bring in some sketchy people, not that I'm discriminating, but when the parks shut down for things like a drought, some people just think it's a free for all." She shrugged. "That's all."

"I couldn't help but notice you jumped on the phone the other day when I was in here and told you about the possible shutdown due to the drought. Who did you call?"

She jerked her head up with a seedy look in her eyes.

"Now, Mae West, you've been hanging around." She stopped herself and slid her eyes Queenie's way. She lifted a brow. "Them too long," she finished her sentence.

"They're good gals." I joked and gave her a look like I fully expected her to tell me the answer. "So?"

"I was talking to my sister. She's been looking at expanding the Cookie Crumble into other small towns around the park and I'd been a little apprehensive. If there's a shutdown here, we'll be in trouble and not be able to stay open." She looked down the counter where the customers were ready to give their order. "I'll be with you in a minute," she told them. "With the new businesses coming, we'll file for the grants the park offers during the shutdown, but with Skip Toliver opening the canoeing and whitewater business, the mayor will sign off on that one for sure. If we'd known about the shutdown, we probably wouldn't've made the mayor her own cookie, because it's not going to be good for us."

I pointed to one of the chocolate sprinkle donuts in the case in front of us. She snapped a white parchment paper from the box and reached in to get the donut, placing it in the bag.

"There's grants?" I sure did have a lot to learn about owning a business in a national park. Not that I wanted to take away from anyone else's business, but I sure would like to keep mine open and a grant would be nice if things did go south.

"I asked Corbin about the shutdown and he didn't want to talk about it. He got all fidgety and there was some aggravation. At first I thought it was because all them inmates were in here with the Normal Baptist Church and they were about to go in the park to pick up trash." Something flickered in her eye. "He was really good at his job."

"You said at first you thought. Then what did you really think?" I encouraged her to finish her sentence after she'd lost her train of thought.

"When I heard he died, I immediately thought of the drought and . . ." she hesitated, "when you're in the food business, you hear people talking while they are deciding what to buy and it really seemed as if the Chamber of Commerce meeting had taken a detour after someone brought up the drought. There were all sorts of fussing and carrying on about getting rid of Corbin and if the mayor didn't do it, they'd figure it out."

"Do you know who said that?" My jaw dropped. Maybe Corbin did die from peanut butter but not by choice.

"I was fixing the display of cookies I'd been asked to bring and I had bent down under the table getting napkins and some business cards." Her face reddened. "I hate to admit it, but I stayed under there listening as in eaves-dropping."

"Was it a woman or man?" I asked.

"Man, though I didn't recognize the voice." That wasn't going to help me any. "When I noticed they'd stopped talking, I slowly got up to see who on earth was saying all that, not that I was going to repeat it or anything. I didn't do me no good, they'd done walked off." She shrugged.

The customers were pacing up and down the counter.

"I've got to go help them." She hurried down the display cases and helped them.

Queenie looked at my donut.

"How did you get that so fast?" She asked.

"I knew what I wanted. Did you go to the Chamber of Commerce meeting last month?" I asked.

"I had a Jazzercise Strike class to teach. I did hear it was a doozie. And I'm definitely going to the one tonight." She continued to look at the chocolate sprinkle donut that I had nestled in the parchment paper and ready to eat.

"Let's go together. I think we've got some information to look into." I handed her the donut, giving it to her and made my way down to where Christine and the customers were finishing up.

I gave them a sweet smile as they passed on the way out the door.

"Christine, can I ask you one more question?" I thought if I did the southern charm girly thing, she'd not catch on that I was trying to piece together the murder of Alison and what I still believed to be the murder of Corbin.

"Sure. I'm going to clean up a bit." She scurried around the counter, grabbing the broom and dust pan from the corner. She swept up the dried leaves that'd fluttered through the door when the customers left.

"You said something about the inmates coming in with Betts and Lester. Do you remember this one?" I dug down in my purse where I'd put Stanley's mugshot.

"That's Stanley Bayer. I've known them all my life." She laughed. "They've always given their poor mama a fit. My mama and daddy told me to stir clear away from the Bayer boys. My sister, well, she's another story. Anyways, I'd heard he was in jail but he wasn't with them the day they came into the bakery."

"Are you sure?" I asked because I remember Betts saying he was in the group.

"As sure as shinola I'm sure." She exuded confidence. "I'da talked to him if he was. We don't have no animosity between us or nothing."

"Why would you?" I asked.

"His mama claimed it was her donut recipe that my sister stole to start our business. I'm not saying Snookie didn't help Mallory out in-home economics class when we were going through school, with a little extra salt here and there, but she certainly didn't steal no full recipe." She continued to sweep.

"I'd heard about that down at the Cute-icle years ago," Queenie said with a mouthful of donut.

"Yep." Christine nodded. "Queenie can tell you all about it."

"You can do that on the way over to see Ardine." I turned back to Christine. "Can I get an apple turnover to go?"

"I'll give you a couple." She winked and got the desserts for me.

Normal wasn't a big town. In fact, it was small, but the county was large and the roads through and in the park were long and windy. I'd yet to figure my way around the entire town since everything I needed was either downtown or at Happy

Trails. Queenie used the pointing method and down yonders to get me to Corbin Ashbrook's house. It was no big shock to see that he lived in an A-frame house, nestled in the woods.

Ardine was sitting on the small deck when we drove up. She looked a little cautious but when she saw Queenie she waved and smiled.

"Ardine, I'm so sorry about Corbin." Queenie dripped with sympathy. It was the first time I'd ever heard her have such deep emotion. Apparently, she and Ardine had been friends a long time because the two embraced and did a lot of nodding as though they were speaking their own language.

"Did he not have his medication on him?" Queenie asked her once they pulled apart.

Ardine's eyes slid over to me.

"I'm sorry," Queenie hand palmed her face. "Where are my manners? This is Mae West."

"I've heard Corbin talk about you." Ardine smiled. "He said you're doing a fine job at Happy Trails."

"Thank you." I sucked in a deep breath as the pain on her face stung my heart. "I'm very sorry for your loss."

"I understand that you found him." She really did recognize me, and I wondered if she was going to ask me questions about it, but she didn't. "I'm glad you did and he didn't stay missing for days." She shook her head. "We always joked that the park would eventually take him. He loved it out there and it was his happy place."

"What about the medication?" I asked, because I thought it was a great question from Queenie.

"He got a call about a missing camper, I believe from Happy Trails. He took off and left his EpiPen along with his cell phone. I didn't think anything of it. He hadn't had a reaction in years. I'm not sure where he got the peanut butter," her voice trailed off and she looked into the distance.

"We brought you an apple turnover from the Cookie Crumble." I held the bag up.

"Those girls sure are good to him." She took the bag and opened it. "There are a few in here. Would y'all like a cup of coffee and enjoy one with me?"

"I'd love it." Queenie was quick to answer.

"Girls?" I asked and we followed her into the A-Frame.

"Christine and Mallory Watson. Both very nice gals. He loved going in there to get his special cookie from Christine on Fridays." Her voice echoed around open timbers of the house.

There was a loft on top and a set of wooden stairs on the right that lead up to it. The kitchen was on the opposite wall while the rest of the open space was filled with furniture facing the wall of windows on the back side with the most amazing view of the Daniel Boone National Park. It was breathtaking.

"Christine wasn't there on Friday. First time in a long time she wasn't." Queenie sat down in one of the stools at the concrete kitchen counter waiting for her apple turnover and coffee.

"She wasn't there?" I asked.

"Nope. It was Mallory. She's not as nice as Christine, but they are both good girls. It's just that Christine goes the extra mile for the customers."

"Do you know if Corbin got his special cookie yesterday morning?" I asked Ardine.

"He sure did. He came home and said that he stopped by there and got his cookie. That was right before he got the call about your camper and headed right out." Ardine slid a cup of coffee across the counter.

"I've got to go." I looked at Queenie. "Come on."

"I'm enjoying my visit with Ardine," she protested.

"I'll take you back," said Ardine. "I've got to go to the funeral home to make some arrangements and I'd love the company on the way into town." Ardine's face was somber as she spoke about the funeral home and the task at hand.

"Are you sure?" I asked.

"Positive." She leaned over the counter and patted Queenie's hand. "We've been friends a long time, ain't we?"

"Mmhhhh. Through a lot together too." Queenie nodded.

"Do you think you could give me the address of Stanley Bayer's mama?" I asked Queenie before I left.

"You just need to take a left out of my driveway and after the hairpin curve, you'll take a sharp right at the fork in the road. Go past three barns and at the fourth barn - it's red - you'll take a right and it's the first trailer on the right." Ardine's hand swiveled around in front of her like it was a car.

Why couldn't these people give house numbers or real directions? I wondered to myself on my way out of the A-frame and into the Escort.

"Hairpin curve, right at fork, fourth barn right, and first trailer on right," I repeated over and over until I got to the trailer. It was nothing like I thought it was going to be.

There were chicken coops, but all the chickens were running free around the trailer that'd seen much better days. There was a goat and a donkey alongside of the house that didn't even look at me when I pulled up.

I questioned why I was here and realized I was probably in over my head in the snooping department. There was one thing I really needed to do before I went in to talk to Snookie.

Call Hank.

"May-bell-ine," his deep southern voice teased me. "To what do I owe the pleasure?"

"I think you're right about Corbin's death being accidental." I heard an audible groan come from him. "I know you told me that my investigating for you was over, but I did get some news."

"And what might that be?" he asked.

"I'd gone to the Cookie Crumble to pick up Ardine an apple turnover," I started to tell my story.

"Why would you go see Ardine Ashbrook when she told me she'd never met you after I told her you were the one who found her husband." He really didn't leave any stone unturned in his investigations.

"I wanted to give her my condolences." Of course I didn't tell him the truth. "Do you want to hear what I have to say or not?"

"Go on."

"Anyways, Christine Watson made Corbin a cookie every Friday morning before she started to bake for the day. This way it couldn't be contaminated with even the slightest of peanut butter. Well, I went in there and she said that Corbin didn't pick up his cookie because it was still sitting on the counter in a baggie. But Ardine said he did go in and get a cookie from Mallory because Christine wasn't there when he showed up." It really did fit like a puzzle. "I think Mallory gave him a cookie that maybe wasn't peanut butter but had somehow been contaminated with peanut butter."

"Is that it?" He didn't sound impressed.

"Ardine also said that he came home and got the call from Dottie about William Hinson. Corbin rushed out of the house and left his EpiPen and cell phone, which I'm sure you already knew since you're the big detective and all." I was kinda proud of myself.

"I did know he left his stuff at home and you might be right about all this. The coroner did say anaphylactic shock could take up to an hour to kick in. He looked like he was on his way back down the trail from his position and couldn't make it back to his truck. The inhaler DNA did come back and it was his DNA. He must've kept it in the ranger pack he wore because the contents had been used a long time ago and there was nothing in it to help him." He paused. "Good work, Mae. I'll check with Mallory. Just so you know, we are closing his case."

"Even though you don't know how he got the peanut butter?" I asked.

"The final contents of his stomach will show exactly what he ate, but there's nothing that points to a homicide." There was a disappointment in his voice. "I just hate that Corbin died like that. He was such a good guy and I really enjoyed working for him."

I listened to Hank tell me a couple of stories about their time together. It was actually heartwarming to hear him recall the fond memories.

"But we must move on with the real murder investigation. Just because we closed Corbin's case doesn't negate the fact there is a murderer out there," he said. "But that's not for you to worry that curly head of hair of yours. You need to take care of Fifi and yourself. I'll go talk to Mallory."

"Are you sure you don't need my help?" I asked right before the buzzer of my phone alarm sounded the reminder of my hair appointment at Cute-icles in an hour, giving me enough time to talk to Snookie, who was staring at me from the front porch with a shotgun at her side.

"Positive. Keep me posted about Fifi because my granny wants a puppy." We said our goodbyes and hung up.

"What you wunt?" Snookie lifted the gun for good measure.

"I'm Mae West and your son was on my trail when he darted out of my campground, Happy Trails." If I'd hadn't just talked to Hank, I'd probably just pulled out of the driveway since it was obvious Stanley wasn't part of the Corbin's death.

"You some cop too?" She asked and sat the butt of the gun back on the porch of the trailer.

"Heck, no. I just wanted to see if you knew where Stanley was. I'm not going to turn him in or nothing. But our park ranger died from natural causes and I wanted to know if Stanley had seen him." I shrugged. "That's all."

"That man was killed?" She asked, her face scrunched.

"No, ma'am. He had some peanut butter and he was allergic to it." It was the simplest answer. "Corbin was a great ranger and we are just piecing together his final hours. That's all."

"Well, you're too late. Stanley was here. He saw the man dead. He took off in fear the fuzz was going to pin this man's death on him since he was a petty thief." She at least told me the truth, which did give me some comfort.

"Did he say if he saw anything fishy or unusual? I have a camper missing and I'm new to the area. I don't know the trails as well as you locals. I'd love to know if he saw any other hikers on the trail." I was amazed at how that popped into my head.

"I'm sure the cops will question him up and down, so you'll have to ask them." She lifted her chin in the air and drew the gun up, cradling it in both arms.

"Cops?" I wasn't sure I heard her correctly.

"Yep. I made him turn himself in a couple hours ago. Normal Police Department. I dropped him off myself and watched with my own two eyes as he walked into the door." She glared at me.

"You're a good mother, Snookie Bayer. Thank you for your time." I waved at her and got back into my car.

She didn't wave back.

CHAPTER 12

With all the yonders, barns and hairpin curves, I finally found my way back to Normal. It just so happened that I turned on the road where the Daniel Boone National Park office was located.

I drove by and noticed the flag at half-staff that I was sure was in honor of Alison. There weren't any cop cars. Even though Agnes told me they'd wrapped up, it was an altogether different scene than the night before.

I turned the Escort around and pulled into the parking lot, looking at the window that was now boarded up. A chill ran up my spine at the thought of someone standing there pointing a gun at her.

I wondered if Alison had survived, would she continue to snoop and uncover what she thought was a big scoop. Or would she say her life was more important. Knowing her the little bit that I did, I couldn't help but think she'd continue with investigating what she'd held secret because she was so passionate about her career.

Not that I wanted to defy what Hank had told me about not sticking my nose into things, I really wanted to see for myself if all the clues were gathered. Going against my own better judgment, I got out of the car and walked right on into the office like I was the boss.

"Hi, Ms. West." The receptionist must've recognized me from the last time I'd been here. Her eyes had a red ring around them, her face was blotchy, and her brown hair looked as if a cat had been sucking on it. It was a much different look than the last time I'd seen her, but she was grieving and it probably took everything she had to come to work. "I didn't think you'd show up today."

"You knew I was coming?" I asked.

"Yes. It's written in Alison's calendar. Since you found her, I assumed you knew the appointment was canceled." She held up the paper calendar. "I've been calling all her appointments to cancel."

Ahem, I cleared my throat and tried to think of a good excuse to get a look at the calendar.

"As you can imagine, I was in such a shock last night after cradling Alison in my lap, that I think I left my purse in the room. I went to the police station and they said they didn't see it." I pointed. "Agnes Swift told me they'd cleared the scene and released the office, so do you mind going back there and looking for me?"

"You can go back." She put a finger in the air. "Mayor MacKenzie, this is Tandy, Alison Gilbert's assistant. I wanted to call and formally let you know that the meeting she has on her calendar with you is canceled. If you have any questions, you can call me back at the Daniel Boone National Park office."

The mayor? The sound of her name hit my gut. In my head, I scanned down the names on the pad of paper I had sitting on the passenger side in the Escort. The only two suspects I had left on the list were William and the mayor.

"I really don't want to go back there. I don't think I'm ready." I blinked a few times, frowning. "Do you mind just going back there to look? I'll wait here."

"Sure." She nodded and frowned too.

Her chair squeaked when she got up. She gave me another tight-lipped smile before she walked down the hall. Quickly, I peeked around the corner and once she was halfway down to the conference room, I grabbed my phone out of my back pocket and touched the camera icon. There was no way I could take the calendar, but I could take several photos of it. I did. I flipped three months back and two months ahead. There was a big red circle around the meeting Alison was going to have with the Mayor. It was the only time that she used red. In my head, it made it stand out to me which told me she knew something about the Mayor. My name was written in pencil, so I knew where I stood. Easily erased.

"I didn't see anything." Tandy came back up right after I took the last few photos of the contacts Alison had listed in the back of her calendar.

"Maybe Hank did pick it up and didn't remember." I let out a long sigh. "I guess I should call him back to double check. Thanks anyways."

"If I find it, I'll let you know." Tandy went back to looking through the calendar as I let myself out.

There was still about twenty minutes until my hair appointment and while I waited in front of Cute-icles in the Escort, I texted Dottie to check on Fifi.

Me: Hey, Dottie. How is Fifi? I texted her.

Dottie: She's is pitiful. I called the vet and she came out. She said it could be any day.

Me: Do I need to come home? I don't mind canceling this hair appointment.

Dottie: Heck no! (scissor emoji followed up by a kissing face) Fifi is fine. I hate texting. Goodbye.

I had to trust that Dottie would let me know if I needed to come home. I dragged the pad of paper from the passenger seat and got a pen out of my purse along with my phone. I crossed Alison off the initial list as well as Stanley. Hank had mentioned something about Jamison and Penelope being each other's alibis, so I crossed them off the list. I couldn't cross the Mayor off the list. She was my choice of suspect for who killed Alison. How was I going to prove that? Confront the Mayor? She'd bring me down if she wanted to. All this meant was that I was going to have to be sly on how I proceeded from here. The information I needed was going to have to be something really big for her to have killed Alison.

The alarm on my phone rang five minutes before my hair appointment. Instead of heading into the salon, I pulled out my phone and used my fingers to blow up the photos I'd taken of Alison's calendar. There was an S.T. on every Friday with a heart around it but the last two Fridays were scribbled out. Now, I'm not cupid, but I did know that when you put hearts around anything, it must be out of love.

The time on the top of my phone showed noon and I didn't want Helen being mad at me for being late. The sleuthing was going to have to wait until Helen used her supposed magic touch on my curly head of hair.

The inside of Cute-icles was Pepto Bismol pink. There was a white flocked Christmas tree in the back with all sorts of camping ornaments on it. She had strung twinkly lights all over the ceiling and all four puffy pink salon chairs had occupants.

"You must be Mae," the young woman behind the counter smiled. "We've been waiting all day for you to get here." She twirled around. "Girls! Girls!" she yelled above the chatter to shush them. "This here is Mae West. She's the one who found both bodies."

"I. . .um . .I. . ." I felt my face redden as a couple of the women in the pink salon chairs rushed over, both of their heads covered in tin foil.

"We can't wait to hear all about it. I'm Pam Purcell." She tugged my arm to drag me over to the chair she was sitting in.

"You're the one with the good apples." I thought I throw her a compliment.

"No, she's not. I'm the only one around here with good fruit. Now who said she had good apples?" The other lady's face squished.

"You must be Carol Wise, with the best peaches." I noted, making her swell with pride.

"The one and only." She perked up a little.

Each woman stood on a side of my chair, bickering about who had the better fruit. Pam's hair was short from what I could tell underneath all the foils and it looked to be silver. She was about half a foot taller than Carol and half a foot wider. She wasn't a big woman, maybe five feet six, but her voice was louder than Carol's squeakier voice that held more southern sarcasm, which I could tell was getting under Pam's skin. Carol, on the other hand, had longer hair that mostly stuck out the ends of her foil. The black long strands stood out.

"What are you looking at?" Carol put her hands on her thin hips and jutted to the side.

"Your hair. What are you doing to it?" I questioned.

"Lowlights for the fall. I come in here each season and get a little fix me up." She winked.

I instantly liked Pam and Carol. They were just good folk that took pride in their businesses.

"Have the two of you ever put your fruit together in mini-pies?" I asked. They looked between each other like I was nuts. "I own Happy Trails Campground and I love featuring all the local businesses. The Cookie Crumble supplies the donuts and some cookies in the morning. The Sweet Smell Flower Shops has a package for our romantic getaways where fresh bouquets of local flowers are in their campers or bungalows waiting for them. That's just to name a few." I could see they were thinking about my idea. "If the two of you put together mini pies with a combined filling of your fruits, I know my campers would love it during our campfire nights. Or you can even hold some sort of pie baking class for some of the ladies."

"Can we get back to you on that?" Carol asked.

"Take your time. I'm not planning to go anywhere." I fell in love with the idea of having some sort of craft or baking class for the campers like we did during the kids' summer camp.

"There's my masterpiece." Helen pushed through the door from the back wall. Her hair was an even brighter orange than the day before. She had on a pink apron to match the inside of her shop. "How do you like my shop?" She asked, plunging her fingers in my curls and brushing them down.

"It's pink." I looked at her in the mirror on the wall in front of my chair.

"My favorite color." She twirled the chair around and started fluffing the top of my scalp with her fingers. "It inspires me. Now, do you trust me?"

"That's a loaded question," I said and wondered what she was thinking.

"I'm gonna put some relaxer on those curls and you just might look like a movie star like your name sake." Her head rotate around and looked at me from all angles. "Why don't you go on and tell us what happened with Alison Gilbert."

They all leaned at the same time with their ears pointed towards me.

"She and I had a meeting. When I showed up she'd been shot." It was simple as that.

"I heard you saw the killer," Pam chirped.

"I heard you gave her CPR," Carol had to put in her two-cents.

"None of those things are true." I had to laugh. "Literally, I walked in, yelled her name and walked to the conference room where the light was on."

Then it hit me. These ladies apparently heard a lot of things. Granted, they were lies, but somewhere there had to be some truth.

"I guess I just won't know what she was investigating that I think got her. . ." I hesitated. They leaned a little closer. "Killed," I whispered with exaggeration.

A collective gasp came from them.

"What was it? Do you know?" The receptionist asked me.

"I'm not sure but I think it had something to do with the Chamber of Commerce meeting last month." I looked up at Helen as she worked on my curls. "Did you go to that meeting?"

"I did." She tucked her bottom lip with her top teeth, her brows lowered, her eyes looked to the right as though she were thinking. "It was the luncheon for the last part of the fiscal year. There was a motion for Skip Toliver to open his new business and use some of the grant money, but I think they voted that down."

"He did start the business. He dropped off some of his business cards at the campground office to drum up business." I had completely forgotten to get Abby to send some social media love his way.

"He did?" Pam's jaw dropped. "With what money?" she asked. "He better not have used those grants. That's something me and you could use for our new fruit business."

"What new fruit business?" Helen asked her.

"The one me and Carol are thinking about starting and if I recall, the applications for the local grants aren't due until the end of the year." Pam tapped her temple.

They rattled on about the prospect of having this grant money for their businesses and Helen threw in her ideas, while I continued to think about Skip and his sister. Helen continued to slap stuff on my hair and the other stylists had taken Pam and Carol's tin foil off their heads, finishing them up. I sat there letting Helen do her magic while they went from one gossip tale to the next, eventually coming back to the possible fruit business Pam and Carol might open.

Helen started the hairdryer and used the round brush on my long hair.

"Speaking of business," Helen had turned off the hair dryer. "What about the drought? We seen the paper and even heard about your missing camper."

"I've not heard anything about the drought. I thought Alison might've been investigating it and that's what got her into hot water, but now that I'm thinking about it, I think she might've been investigating the grant money Skip Toliver. . ." My mouth slammed shut.

"Are you okay?" Helen covered my eyes with her hand and sprayed the hairspray all over my hair.

"Skip Toliver. S.T." I gasped. "Is Skip married?"

"Heck, no. Who'd want him?" She twirled me around to look in the mirror. "Well, what do you think?"

"I think Alison Gilbert wanted him." I looked at my reflection in the mirror, not recognizing that the beauty with long, straight hair was me. The depths of my eyes confirmed it was me and also told me that Alison Gilbert's every Friday night date was with Skip Toliver.

CHAPTER 13

The more I thought about Skip being the S.T. in Alison's calendar, the more my brain calculated exactly why Mayor MacKenzie would kill her.

Because of the Mayor's own words, that I'd heard with my own ears when she and Corbin were trying to get William Hinson under control at the Happy Trails party, when she implied there was not going to be a shutdown. If Alison was dating Skip, she'd have firsthand knowledge of any and all information about the grants since he was the one applying for them and ultimately the Mayor was the one who had to sign off on them. Since the year was almost over and we all knew the economy slowed down in the winter months, if she could force Corbin to hold off on declaring the drought, then we'd be past the economy's busy seasons and at the deadline for Skip's canoe business to really be taking off. But, the grant sure would help him get some marketing set up over the winter months for a big spring campaign that'd bring in even more money for Normal. More money than any other sort of shop since it was the hiking and outdoor activities that initially brought the tourists here. Alison's calendar with the crossed-out hearts added up. The first crossed out heart was the week before last. Was it a coincidence that Skip came into the Happy Trails office and said that his Fridays had been freed up? I didn't think so.

Alison had to have caught on to the idea that the Mayor was abusing her powers and started to investigate. Of course, Alison shared it with Skip who in turned told his sister. They are family and around here. . . blood was thicker than thieves. The Mayor couldn't risk it coming out, so the only way to silence Alison's determined drive was to silence her permanently.

The courthouse was only open until noon on Saturdays but didn't even open today since it was Labor Day weekend, which meant that the Mayor wasn't going to be in her office. Skip's business was open. He even said he was open seven days a week.

There was a lot of accusing in my theory and it could bring down the entire Normal government if not handled properly. This I knew was something that was over my head and I was going to have to tell Hank about it.

I whipped the Escort back around and headed out of town towards the police station. Even though it was included in the courthouse, they didn't close. I probably drove faster than I should've, but was relieved to see Hank's big black car parked up to the building. I parked in the space next to him.

"Can I help you?" Agnes pulled the window open.

"Agnes? You're working on the holiday weekend?" I asked.

"Mae, is that you under that fancy straight hair?" Her

jaw dropped. "Why you look like one of them fancy models." She jerked her head around. "Hank, you better get over here and get a gander at Mae West before she turns the head of every man, married or eligible, in Normal."

"Granny," Hank said her name with an exhausted sigh before he looked through the window. "Mae," his voice trailed off.

When his green eyes looked at me, there was a softness in them I'd never seen before that made my pulse skitter alarmingly. My skin prickled.

"Umm. . . He gulped.

"Don't she look so pretty?" Agnes nudged him.

"What's up?" He ignored her. Again, one of those manners he could've used, which he didn't. A girl likes to be complimented.

"I've got some information I'd like to share with you about Alison Gilbert's murder." I drew my shoulders back. My voice was strong.

The buzz of the door sounded to the left of me, signaling that Agnes had unlocked the door to get into the station from the entrance.

Hank met me on the other side and gestured for me to walk down the hall towards the interrogation rooms. Silently and once we made it to the first room, he opened the door and walked in, me behind him.

He could've opened the door for me, telling my flip-flopping heart that he wasn't the gentleman Ty was.

"I hope you didn't go snooping for it and it somehow fell into your lap." He did actually pull one of the chairs out for me before he walked around the table to take a seat in the chair facing mine.

"You aren't going to like it, but," I said and took my

phone out to show him Alison's calendar. "I'm not sure if Alison had a calendar on her computer or phone, but I do know that her handwriting says a lot."

I slid my phone across the table for him to look at. He swiped the screen, blew up the photos, and after a few minutes sat the phone down.

"Tandy the receptionist at the park office," I started to say.

"I know Tandy. I work there when I'm on Ranger duty." His face was still and serious.

"Anyways, she was making calls to the appointments on the calendar to cancel since Alison won't be attending." I tried to honor her in my words the best way I could. "If you noticed the hearts around the initials S.T. and then they are scribbled out."

"I did." He nodded.

"I think Alison was going to uncover some corruption with the Mayor and her brother." My words were met with an uneasy wiggling from him in his chair. After all, the Mayor was the boss of the police department and the detectives, making this a very serious accusation on my part. "Hear me out."

Over the next twenty minutes Hank sat there silent and emotionless as I told him what I'd uncovered. The more I heard it out loud, the more it made complete sense.

"It might not be big corruption, but enough that if Alison uncovered it, the Mayor wouldn't be elected next term and we all know Courtney MacKenzie wants to be re-elected," I said, sitting back into the chair and waiting for him to say something.

Anything.

My face reddened as the silence went on between us. My

hands started to sweat. I tapped my fingers on my legs just waiting.

"I'll look into it," was all he said about my theory before he stood up. "Do you have a hot date with Ty?"

"What?" I snorted. "You mean to tell me that I'm handing you the killer and all you can think about is Ty?" Unbelievable. I stood up and threw my hands in the air. "I don't know what beef you and Ty have other than Nicki Swaggert, but you're a grown man that needs to move on with his personal life."

I continued to shake my head in disbelief. I'd completely wasted my time coming to talk to him when I should've just gone to the police and not to the detective. But I thought I was doing the right thing.

"Before you go, I think you should know that Jamison and Penelope's alibi checks out. They said they went out to eat, that was verified through bank statements because he used a credit card, and Bobby Ray Bond saw them go into the bungalow and not come out until the next morning when they saw William," he said to my back as I was walking down the hall.

"I thought you said Corbin's death was accidental." I jerked around and glared at him.

"I'm not talking about Corbin. I'm talking about William Hinson. He's still missing and the ranger station sent out search and rescue on him overnight near the downtown trails since it was where he was last seen. I couldn't help but wonder if Jamison and Penelope had something to do with his disappearance since they are in love." He chuckled. "You know how that whole three-person love triangle gets a little messy."

I blinked a few times wondering what on earth he was

talking about, but he left me standing there at the end of the hallway.

"Mae West," Agnes chirped from behind me. I turned around. "Three-person triangle. You, Ty and Hank." She winked. "You just might get more than a coffee date out of him yet."

CHAPTER 14

"Was he talking about me?" I asked myself over and over again about what Hank had said about the three-person triangle.

There was no making sense of that man. If he wasn't going to check out my theory. I was sure going to hike right on down to the river off Red Fox Trail and confront Skip Toliver myself.

I'd never in my life driven so fast to get back to the campground. I was rushing against the clock for daylight hours to hike down the trail, talk to Skip, and get back up the trail.

"Can I help you?" Dottie Swaggert didn't recognize the newly coiffed straight hair that Helen had actually worked magic on.

"It's me, Mae!" I hollered back from where I'd parked the car up to the trail. "New hair! I'm going down to see Skip. If I'm not back in an hour, you come get me!"

"Wait!" She walked across the campground. "I'm supposed to tell you to meet Ty at the waterfall."

"Waterfall?" I asked.

"Yes." She bent over to catch her breath from her hurrying over to me.

"See there." I shook a finger at her. "That's from smoking."

"Your rowdy friends from Bungalow Five left this afternoon." She was getting really good at ignoring my jabs at her smoking habit. "I guess they went from search and rescue for William to just a rescue mission."

"Hank told me he released them." I turned back to the trail.

"Listen, Ty didn't want me to tell you, but he planned a romantic picnic at the waterfall for the two of you. I went into your camper and got your bathing suit. He's got it." She grinned. "He's trying to woo you, Mae."

I was trying to solve a case, though I didn't tell her that.

"The waterfall is just across from where Skip has set up one of the checkpoints for his business, so after you see him for whatever it is you want, just walk over there. Don't leave that poor boy alone and waiting." Dottie didn't say it, but I could tell she knew I was struggling with something or someone that I couldn't bring myself to even comprehend.

"How's Fifi?" I asked.

"She's fine. I did give her some chicken from the campfire when she didn't want to eat her kibble. She gobbled it right up." Dottie patted me on the back. "Now, go have fun. Let loose. You deserve it after the few days you've had. And that hair is great."

"Helen really did a good job." I filled my lungs with a big deep breath of the fresh fall air and headed up the trail.

As much as I wanted to be excited for what Ty had done for me and what was waiting for me at the waterfall, I was actually angry at Hank for not even giving me a compliment on my hair. It was such a girl thing, but he knew. Where were his manners?

The more steps along the trail I took, the angrier I got, and the beautiful fall foliage couldn't even bring me out of it. It wasn't until I noticed Skip sitting in a canoe on really dry land did I see that there was a big drought.

"No customers?" I asked from the top of the trail that descended down to him.

"Can't you see that it's a bit dry?" He gave the two-finger wave over his head. "Corbin Ashbrook was right. The drought is among us. I had to give back all the deposits from tourists because the water isn't deep enough for even a canoe."

"I hate to hear that." This was the first time that I truly got scared about Happy Trails and the reservations. I gulped back the thoughts and got to the matter at hand. "I'm actually here to talk to you about all of this."

I pointed to the few canoes and rafts for the rapids he'd put on the banks in his makeshift business.

"I'm listening." He patted the space in the canoe next to him for me to sit down, but I wanted to stand.

"Where you dating Alison Gilbert?" It seemed like a good place to start before I accused his sister for killing her.

"Yep. She went to great lengths to make sure we had really fun Fridays together. It was her only day off because she said big news always broke on the weekends. She was a lot of fun. I even thought she was the one until she dumped me a couple of weeks ago," his voice cracked. "Now she's gone."

There was visible pain in his eyes as they teared up. My heart sank.

"I know this is going to sound awful, but Alison was my friend. I feel obligated to find out who killed her and why.

She told me about the grant money and how your sister wanted Corbin to drag his feet on closing down the park due to an impending drought."

"She told you that?" He stood up and used the back of his hand to brush away the loose tears down his cheek. "I filled out that grant paperwork like everyone else who filed for it. My business would bring in young people, not just lifetime RVers and families that like to camp. If the millennials come here, they will come for generations. Normal has nothing like this to cater to them."

"You're a millennial."

"That's why I know. I'm so bored around here. All my friends have moved away. On to better things. When I went out to Colorado to visit my buddy, he opened one of these and it's thriving in their state parks." He had a point. "That's what I want to bring to Normal. Is my sister wrong for wanting the same thing? A great life for all the citizens here? So maybe my paperwork went to the top of the pile? So what."

"You don't think Alison's uncovering that would hurt your sister's status as our Mayor? Giving favors to family?" I asked, seeing both sides of the argument.

"Are you saying that you think my sister killed Alison because Alison was trying to become some big investigative reporter who thought she had some sort of story on corruption in the Mayor's office?" He asked and laughed at the same time.

"It's possible." I shrugged, not finding him so funny. "Alison was passionate about her job. She told me that something big was coming down the pipeline."

"That was Alison's problem. She's. . .was a millennial like the rest of our friends. One big story that'd get her noticed and she was out of Normal too. Do you honestly think she wanted to write for the Normal Gazette and spend her life sending articles to the National Parks of America Magazine in hopes they print her article? No. She had bigger plans. She didn't care how all the facts fit together, just as long as her name got noticed." He shook his head in disappointment. "Besides, my sister and I were at my father's eightieth birthday party all night. She rented out the Normal Diner for it. Ask your boyfriend." He nodded to the right where Ty had appeared.

"Mae, you coming to find me?" Ty had a big smile on his face.

"I am." I smiled back, though I was sorting out all the accusations I'd told Hank and now Skip about the Mayor.

"Did your family have a good night at your dad's birthday?" Ty asked Skip. "My dad said it was fun."

"We had a great time. We thanked your dad, but please let him know again how much fun it was." Skip looked at me with a blank stare.

I walked over to Ty.

"What was that about?" He asked about the cold shoulder Skip was giving me, the one I so rightly deserved.

"Nothing. Just talking about the drought," I looked up at him. "Dottie sent me to look for you," I said, looking over at him.

There was a slight hesitation in his hawk-like eyes.

"Your hair." He ran his hand down a few strands of my hair. "Where's your curls?"

"You don't like it?" I asked, figuring I'd get the same reaction from him as I've gotten from everyone else I've seen since I got it done.

"It's pretty. You're pretty no matter what you do to your hair, but your curls make you stand out. That's all." His hand slipped past my shoulder and down my arm, taking my hand in his.

All of my emotions had found a spot right at the base of my throat. I wanted to scream. I'd gone from investigating Corbin's murder to it not being a murder, to finding Alison's murdered body and trying to investigate that, to a totally different hair style that would stay this way for weeks until the solution washed out, to accusing our Mayor of corruption, not to mention the emotions I was battling between a really nice guy and a gruff one.

I swallowed hard a few times as Ty guided me along the banks of the river into the clearing of Red Fox Trail waterfall, the destination for all the hikers that took this trail.

With the first sign of dusk and the last little bit left of the sun's rays, the waterfall had the perfect small rainbows of color starting at the base where it landed in the pool of water. The drought had yet to touch it, but soon this magnificent feature would be dead too until the drought was over.

"Isn't it beautiful?" Ty asked.

"Amazing." The grass around it and the wild ferns were still vibrant along the banks. The limestone in the water was perfect fertilizer.

"I know you've been busy and we've not really gotten to have a real date. Since it's Labor Day weekend, the campground is full, and you're working, I wanted to give you a little dinner before the rush." He knew what it was like not to get to celebrate holidays in our business. It was something we'd gotten used to.

He'd be at the diner cooking while I was making sure the campers had a great holiday vacation.

"I made some shrimp foil packs over the campfire. I know you're going to love it." His words made my mouth water.

"I'm starving. I've not eaten all day." I decided to not even talk about my day and Alison or what I'd found out. None of that seemed important anymore.

Skip all but confirmed that I wasn't a good amateur detective and Ty showed me what life could be like with a pure gentleman.

He'd laid a blanket down on the ground. There was a bottle of wine and two wine glasses nestled inside the picnic basket. While he poured the wine, I opened one of the foil packs. The warmth of the flavors filled my soul. My shoulders fell from my ears, my heart beat normal, and my breathing was back to steady. I was relaxed for the first time all day.

"You devoured that corn on the cob." Ty laughed with joy on his face. "I love seeing you eat my food. It makes me really happy."

"You're such a good chef." I picked up my bathing suit that was lying on the blanket with his trunks. "Let's take a relaxing dip before it's too dark to enjoy."

Obviously, we'd not yet reached the stage in our relationship to change in front of each other, so we took turns going into the woods to change.

I dipped a toe into the water and told myself that I was going to take a cleansing bath in the moonlight waterfall. Come out a renewed girl. Leave the death of Corbin behind and the murder of Alison up the police. My sleuthing days were over along with any sort of feeling I had towards Hank Sharp.

I dove into the water and let it flow down my body. When I came up for air, my hair felt funning laying down my back in a straight line when it was usually springing up around my ears. Ty was like a little kid. He dove and swam around, splashed and flipped.

"Thank you for making tonight so special. You have no idea how much I needed this." I took the initiative to wrap my arms around him.

There was a stirring over his right shoulder. A few bubbles, making me think it was a school of passing fish.

"I was beginning to think we weren't meant to happen," Ty's words floated into my ears, making it seem like a dream as a hand popped up where the bubbles were coming from. It had a fancy watch in its grip just like the fancy watches William Hinson had given his groomsmen. Like a spotlight, the moonbeam highlighted the engraved initials "JTD" as clear as day.

"You tensed. Did you not like what I said?" He turned his head over his right shoulder to see what I was staring at before he grabbed me and dragged me to the shore.

"Is that?" I licked my lips to wet my dry mouth.

"I'll call Hank." The disappointment dripped from his tone as he took one of the beach towels and wrapped it around me.

After Hank and the police had gotten to the crime scene and determined it was in fact William Hinson with bruising around his neck due to an unofficial cause of death by strangulation, Hank let me and Ty leave.

He did tell us that he'd question us after the holiday and try to enjoy the next couple of days. He didn't even make any sort of smart remarks about me and Ty. He was very professional. Ty and I had made it back to the campground and stood in front of my camper in silence.

"Mae," Ty's voice broke. "Since the first day I saw you in Normal, I thought you was the prettiest thing I'd ever laid my eyes on. I've lived in and among this world and I was smitten. Over the last few months since you moved here and

I moved back, forces of nature just aren't letting us get together the way I want to be together."

I could see where this was going. Just another dead thing thrown in my path to end a nutty week.

"You don't have to say anything." I gave him the pass. "I do want you to know that I think you are a true gentleman. I've never been treated so kind by a man in my life."

He laughed and said, "Maybe you need someone a little gruffer around the edges to tame you, Mae West."

I stood there watching as he moseyed on down to his camper and didn't go inside to check on Fifi until I saw him flip on his lights. He wasn't coming back to try to win me over.

CHAPTER 15

"Shhh!!" Betts turned up the TV at the Laundry Club. "They're having a news conference."

There we all sat with our pumpkin spice coffee and donuts in the middle of the Laundry Club on this Labor Day morning. We knew we'd all be too busy to get together to celebrate so we'd decided to get together early, with Fifi in tow.

Fifi looked like she could pop any minute. She was going to have to stick close to me all day because I had a feeling the three littles ones, confirmed by the ultrasound the vet had given Fifi, were going to come into this world any minute now.

There was silence, probably the most silent I'd ever heard the laundromat, as we listened to Hank Sharp talk to the press about William Hinson and how they had Jamison Todd Downey in custody for murder.

"Let me start off by saying," he started out. I couldn't help but notice he had on the same jacket he'd put around my shoulders after I found Alison. The smell came back to me as if it were still around me. "The death of Corbin Ashbrook was not a murder. His death was from eating a cookie that'd been in contact with peanut butter. He was highly allergic to peanuts and he died on a trail that he loved. He will be greatly missed. Mr. William Hinson, the camper who went missing, and reporter Alison Gilbert were murdered by Jamison Downey, who is in custody. Mr. Downey killed Mr. Hinson because of a love triangle he was having with Mr. Hinson's fiancée. Mr. Downey had killed Mr. Hinson in hopes his body would never be found in the depths of the Daniel Boone National Park. Ms. Gilbert made the deadly mistake of telling Mr. Downey that about her theory of corruption within the Normal government, making it seem like Ranger Ashbrook's death was a murder plot. Let me stop here and tell you that there is no corruption within Normal's government." He put his hands up. There were sounds of cameras clicking. "We've investigated that and this packet the news media is going to get outline the facts that show no such wrong doing." He held up the packets and handed them off to Agnes Swift, who then started to distribute them to the news media.

He continued.

"Mr. Downey had placed Mr. Hinson's sweatshirt at Ranger Corbin's place of death on the trail. He admitted in a sworn statement that he wanted us to believe that Mr. Hinson killed Ranger Ashbrook in a fit of rage and then disappeared."

As he spoke, all of the images of Jamison talking to Alison at the campground after we'd found Corbin and the images of watches started to complete the puzzle.

"As for Ms. Gilbert, she'd had a couple of conversations with Mr. Downey that made him, in a psychotic state at the time, believe she knew he'd killed Mr. Hinson and in return he shot her from outside of the Daniel Boone National Park offices. We have recovered the gun and it's in evidence." He was so confident as he spoke and looked dead into the camera.

"You okay?" I bent over and whispered in Fifi's ear as she began to moan and roll to the other side.

"I'm not going to take any questions at this time. All of this is just brand-new information over the last twelve hours. I'll hold another news conference after the Labor Day weekend. Thank you." He turned and walked back into the police station.

"That's crazy," Abby said.

"Are you sure she's okay?" Dottie looked over at Fifi.

Her little pink tongue was out and she was panting. She stood up and started to pace around the laundromat. We followed behind her.

"I think she's trying to find a place to give birth," Betts said.

"Okay, then." Queenie jerked open a dryer that was still on cycle and pulled out a few pieces of clothing, tossing in front of Fifi right before she stepped on them.

"Queenie," Betts scolded. "Those aren't your clothes."

"We need them." Queenie took off to the front of the laundromat, her phone to her ear.

"Who is she calling at this time?" Dottie asked, but I ignored her.

"Can you get her some water to drink or something?" I asked and sat down on the tile floor next to Fifi where she'd laid on the warm clothes.

She'd started to lick her girly parts. Her nipples had grown. The moaning had stopped and she was in birthing mode. For the next ten minutes, she licked her stomach and nuzzled her nose into her belly. We all watched in disbelief.

The door of the Laundry Club swung open and Hank Sharp rushed in.

"Is she okay?" He hurried over, those green eyes staring at me.

"I'm not sure." I gulped, rubbing my hands along my arm to ward off the sudden chill. "How did you know?"

"I called 9-1-1 and told them we were having a baby in the Laundry Club," Queenie joked.

"When the call came through, I texted Queenie and she said it was Fifi, so I came to help." He took off his coat and swung it over my shoulders. He rolled up his button-down shirt sleeves and reared up on his haunches. "I've helped birth many puppies," he assured me with a warm smile. "She's going to be just fine."

In no time, Fifi had pushed out three little pink puppies and had started to lick them clean. We all sat back and watched in amazement. Fifi was a natural at being a mama. Hank's big strong hands rubbed gently over Fifi's face, giving her comfort and love, sending my heart into a frenzy.

"Do you have any soup?" He asked Betts.

"In my office for when I need to heat up something quick. I think I have chicken noodle." She stood up.

"Can you go heat it up and bring the broth for Fifi. She needs something to eat." He looked down at my sweet Fifi. She was still cleaning her babies as they began to nurse.

Tears fell from my eyes.

"You are such a good mama. I'm so proud of you," I whispered in her ear. Hank stood up and walked away letting me be with her.

"Hashtag Fifi had her babies at the hashtag laundry club hashtag detective Hank Sharp delivered the hashtag babies," Abby talked out loud while she pecked away on her phone.

I moved back once Betts had the warm broth. Fifi knew it was for her. She turned just enough so the babies could still eat while she lapped up the warm broth. Exactly what she needed.

Betts held the bowl while the other girls continued to stroke Fifi's back and tell her what a good girl she was.

"Thank you for coming. I'm not sure we'd known what to do," I said once I walked over to the coffee station where Hank was getting a cup of coffee.

He handed me the cup he'd fixed.

"You know, I'm not a jerk. I'm a gentleman, even though you don't think so." Was he trying to convince me of something? "When you're in my job, you become a little harder hearted. I like Ty Randal all right. I've got nothing against him."

"He is a nice guy, just not for me." It was my subtle way of opening the door for whatever Hank might've been eluding to. He might not be the guy who twists the cap off my beer, but he was the man that noticed I was chilled and twice gave me his coat.

"Then I'm going to take you out on a date and show you just how much of a southern gentleman I can be." He didn't leave room for it to be a question. "I'm going to pick you up at 8 o'clock Thursday night. I know you have Fridays off, so be prepared to stay out late."

Hank didn't bother getting himself a coffee or waiting for my answer. He walked out the door of the Laundry Club and didn't look back.

"What was that about?" Dottie Swaggert walked up behind me. Her head tilted to the right and then left to get a look at Hank walking across the street.

"I'm not sure." I tugged the edges of the suit coat up around my nose and took in a big inhale. "But I think it's the security I've always been looking for."

After letting Fifi get some rest, I laid Hank's suit coat down on the passenger side of the Escort and put her and her babies on top of it.

We pulled into the campground. The campers were jumping into the lake and trying to use the pedal boats and getting stuck in some low spots. There was music coming from some of the campers. The campfires were lit and the twinkling lights all plugged in. Drought or no drought, Happy Trails Campground was in full swing and everyone had a smile on their faces. Labor Day had truly turned out to be labor day for Fifi.

When I passed by the lake, Ty turned around. He and his little brother, Timmy, were fishing off the dock. There was a look in his eye that told me he was at peace with the decision he'd made last night and that made me feel good.

I wasn't sure where my love life was going to go, but I did know that me and Ty weren't meant to be right now and my heart was bursting with love for Fifi and her three babies.

Out of nowhere and just as I pulled up to the camper, big drops of rain belted the windshield of my car. I started laughing out loud. Fifi looked up at me. Her small round black eyes were tired.

"We are blessed." I patted her and looked out the rearview mirror.

The campers were dancing in the rain. The drought was about to be over. My heart was full of joy. Once again, Happy Trails Campground was exactly where I needed to be in my life.

It was home.

Want more of Mae West and the Laundry Club Ladies?
The next book in the series, CHRISTMAS, CRIMINALS,
AND CAMPERS, is available to purchase or read in Kindle
Unlimited. CLICK HERE! And read on for a sneak peek.

But wait! Readers ask me how much my cozy mysteries and
the characters in them reflect my real life. Well...here is a
good story for you.

Whooo hooo!! I'm so glad we are a week out from last Coffee
Chat with Tonya and happy to report the poison ivy is
almost gone! But y'all we got more issues than Time magazine up in our family.
When y'all ask me if my real life ever creeps into books,
well...grab your coffee because here is a prime example!
My sweet mom's birthday was over the weekend. Now, I'd
already decided me and Rowena was going to stay there for
a couple of extra days.
On her birthday, Sunday, Tracy and David were there too,
and we were talking about what else...poison ivy! I was
telling them how I can't stand not shaving my legs. Mom
and Tracy told me they don't shave daily and I might've
curled my nose a smidgen. And apparently it didn't go
unnoticed.
I went inside the house to start cooking breakfast for
everyone and mom went up to her room to get her bathing
suit on and Tracy was with me. All the men were already
outside on the porch.
The awfulest crash came from upstairs and my sister tore
out of that kitchen like a bat out of hell and I kept flipping
the bacon. My mom had fallen...shaving her legs!

Great. Now it's my fault.

Her wrist was a little stiff but she kept saying she was fine. We had a great day. We celebrated her birthday, swam, and had cake. When it came time for everyone to leave but me and Ro, I told mom that she should probably go get an x-ray because her wrist was a little swollen.

After a lot of coaxing, she agreed and I put my shoes on and told Tracy, David, and Eddy to go on home and we'd call them.

My mama looked me square in the face and said, "You're going with that top knot on your head?"

I said, "yes."

She sat back down in the chair and said, "I'm not going with you lookin' like that."

"Are you serious?" I asked.

"Yes. I'm dead serious. I'm not going with you looking like that. What if we see someone?" She was serious, y'all!
She protested against my hair!

Now...this is exactly like the southern mama's I write about! I looked at Eddy and he was laughing. Tracy and David were laughing and I said, "I can't wait until I tell my coffee chat people about this."

As you can see in the above photo, the before and after photo.

Yep...we went and she broke her wrist! Can you believe that? We were a tad bit shocked, and I'll probably be staying a few extra days (which will give us even more to talk about over coffee next week).

Oh...we didn't see anyone we knew so I could've worn my top knot! As I'm writing this, you can bet your bottom dollar my hair is pulled up in my top knot!

Okay, so y'all might be asking why I'm putting this little

story in the back of my book, well, that's a darn tootin' good question.

This is exactly what you can expect when you sign up for my newsletter. There's always something going on in my life that I have to chat with y'all about each Tuesday on Coffee Chat with Tonya. <u>I hope you join us by clicking here and signing up.</u>

Chapter One of Book Four
CHRISTMAS, CRIMINALS, AND CAMPERS

"The way Nadine carefully wove the tapestry of the small town really did make it feel like its own character," Abby Fawn said with a deep sigh of happiness. She spoke so fondly of the book she had picked for The Laundry Club's monthly book club meeting.

It was no secret that Abby Fawn was Nadine White's biggest fan. Abby had used her position as a librarian many times to get advance reader copies of Nadine's books before they were published.

"No matter what we say about the book, Abby is going to defend it until she convinces us to feel the same way." Dottie Swaggert curled her nose as though she smelled the dirty laundry a tourist was throwing into the closest washing machine.

The Laundry Club was a full-service laundromat in downtown Normal, Kentucky. It wasn't just a place to do your laundry; it was like nothing you've ever seen. It was upscale, and Betts Hager had done a fabulous job offering the comforts of home for her customers.

Since Normal was located smack dab in the middle of Daniel Boone National Park, it was a tourist destination for campers and hikers who needed a laundry facility. Betts wanted her customers to be as comfortable doing laundry at The Laundry Club as they were in their homes. She set up a coffee and drink bar and offered snacks. She had a sitting area complete with a television and couches. The customers loved to hang around the puzzle area where there was always a jigsaw puzzle to solve. The little library area, where we held our monthly book club meetings, had shelves stocked with books from Abby that the library could no longer use or were too damaged to put on the shelf as well as a computer.

The first time I drove into downtown Normal in my camper, The Laundry Club had been my first stop. And this here is where I'd met these ladies that I now could rely on for anything I ever needed. We'd truly become what the name was - The Laundry Club.

"Do you have something to say about *Cozy Romance in Christmas*?" Abby directed her question to Dottie.

"Nope." Dottie sat back, crossing her arms in front of her. "I thought it could've used a little more oomph if you know what I mean."

"This is a very popular women's fiction book. It was my turn to choose the book and I wanted to pick something that gave us a good and happy feeling inside that we can hold onto during the Christmas season since our next book club won't be until the New Year." Abby jerked her head towards me. Her brown-haired ponytail whipped around her. "Mae? What are your thoughts on the town being its own character?"

"Well." I hesitated by taking a moment to look at the book's cover to get the author's name.

We all knew that Dottie liked her novels a little steamier and Queenie French liked her cowboy romances, but honestly, I preferred a good cozy mystery. Over the past few months I'd even used some tricks I'd learned from my favorite cozy mystery authors to help the local sheriff's department bring a few criminals to justice.

"Um. . . Nadine White does make you feel like you are in the town on the cover." I held the book up with the cover facing outwards. "I love how the snow is falling in front of the yarn shop. It's also cute how the cat is in the display window."

"But what about the friendships Nadine wrote about?" Abby asked.

"If y'all treated me with kid gloves and all that rah-rah we are sisters stuff, I'd think you'd lost your ever-lovin' mind." Dottie didn't waste any time giving her opinion.

"I think it was very nice." Betts Hager was opening The Laundry Club's mail. "No matter what you think, Dottie, our little group has become a much-needed girls' group for me just like the one Nadine created in the book. There were some people with flaws, but it's fiction." She ripped open an envelope and pulled out a letter. "What about you, Queenie?" Betts asked another member of our book club, pushing back a strand of her wavy shoulder length hair and brushing her bangs to the side as she read the letter to herself.

"I'm not saying it was the worst book we've read, but I'm certainly not going to continue with the series." Queenie adjusted the Jazzercise logo headband up over her forehead. Her short blonde hair was sticking straight up like a bunch of matchsticks. She did look great for being in her sixties, but her colorful wardrobe choices could use a little improvement. "There's like twenty books in the series."

Abby Fawn's brows drew down.

"Abby, we all liked it. Just not as much as you." I reached over to give her comfort.

"Guys," Betts Hager put her hands in her lap, gripping the letter. "We all better really like it because Nadine White is coming to our book club."

"What?" Dottie's face pinched.

Abby reached across our circle of chairs and snatched the letter out of Betts's hands.

"I always invite the authors we pick to The Laundry Club book club meetings, never figuring one would show up."

"Oh my Gawd!" Abby shook with excitement. "She's getting ready to write her next novel over the winter and will be in Normal for Christmas. When she looked up Normal on the internet, she noticed all of my social media posts and hashtags. She decided that she's going to check out Happy Trails Campground and rent a camper for the entire winter season to work on her next novel."

"Happy Trails?" That got my attention right away since I was the owner of the tourist destination of choice deep in the Daniel Boone National Park.

Long story short, my now-dead ex-husband had gone to jail for a Ponzi scheme after swindling millions of dollars from people all over the country, including all the women in the book club. When he went to jail, I had no idea he'd named me the sole owner of a rundown campground in Normal, Kentucky, while everything else was his name only and was seized by the government.

Going from the high life in Manhattan to a campground in Normal wasn't my idea of fun or the way I had wanted to spend my life. I'd spent the better part of my teenage years getting out of the Kentucky foster care system after my own family had been killed in a housefire.

It had taken me a few months to get the campground up and running on top of doing many odd jobs around the quaint town of Normal, but I'd made it a success. In doing so, not only did I gain the trust of the citizens that my husband had abused, but I had also brought the tourists back to the sleepy town by offering luxurious camper-style arrangements that were better than any hotel in Daniel Boone National Park.

Over the past couple of seasons, Happy Trails Campground had been used for family reunions, honeymoons, and family outings. I was proud of what I had done and its impact on our small town, and Abby Fawn had worked alongside me by doing her fabulous social media marketing in addition to being the town's librarian.

"I ain't never gotten no call about a Nadine White." Dottie Swaggert reached out to get the letter from Abby. She would know. She and I both lived at the campground. She was the manager and took all the reservations.

"Can I have that letter to keep?" Abby gushed with delight and took her phone out of her pocket. "Hashtag Nadine White is going to join the hashtag The Laundry Club hashtag book club to talk about her hashtag women's fiction hashtag novel hashtag *Cozy Romance in Christmas*."

"Abby!" Betts called out her name when she realized Abby was plastering Nadine White's visit all over social media.

"What was that?" I looked around when the lights in the laundromat flickered.

"The snow." Betts waved it off. "We have overhead powerlines out back that feed the electric and the heavy snow will sit on the line, wreaking havoc with the electricity." She pointed to the television that showed a snowy picture instead of the Weather Channel we had been watching because there was a snowstorm headed our way. "The electricity rarely goes out, but the internet and cable do. Abby," she got Abby to look up from her phone. "You can't put that on social media. In her letter, she specifically states that it's a getaway and no one but her agent will know where she is."

"Oh, no." Abby clicked and swiped away on her phone. "I don't have service."

"You better get service fast because she's coming today." Dottie shoved the letter in my face.

"Today?" My jaw dropped. "We don't have her reservation."

"Not under her name, but under Valerie Young." Dottie poked at the paper with her finger. "That's her agent."

"Valerie Young is the one who requested a Christmas tree and some fun lights around the rental camper." I had just finished putting up the Christmas tree last night in anticipation of her arrival.

"You've got to do more than that," Abby's voice rose with each word as the joy and anticipation over her favorite author's arrival bubbled up within her. "You've got to go all out and decorate the outside too."

"I did see Buck put some new decorations in the display window of the Tough Nickel Thrift Shop." Queenie unzipped the fanny pack that was clasped around her waist and took out an emery board to file a hangnail.

"You've got to do it. Can't you tell how much Nadine loves Christmas from this book?" Abby begged. "I can help. I've read all of her books and there's a few Christmas ones. She loves trees all decorated with colored bulbs and she loves those snowmen blow-ups. Loves them," she emphasized with her hands along with wide open eyes. "I've got to invite her to the library to do a reading." Abby jumped up and started to pace. She'd stop, hold her phone up in the air, look at it, shake it, and do it all over again in an effort to get some cell service. "It's perfect. A Christmas present for Normal."

"I'm not so sure she wants anyone to know she's here." Betts sighed. We all stared at Abby in amazement. She was so giddy and childlike. Granted, she was in her early twenties and the youngest of the group, but this was an author, not some big Hollywood actress.

"No." I put my hand out. That was the last thing she needed to be involved in. I'd never seen Abby this excited, not even since she'd started dating Ty Randal, one of Normal's most eligible bachelors and kinda a suitor of mine when I first moved to Normal. "You've got a lot on your mind and I'm crunched for time to get the camper ready."

"It's her own fault if she didn't tell you to get more decorations up." Dottie tugged her cigarette case out of her front pocket. "Come on, I'll go with ya."

"So it's set." Abby gathered in the middle of us before we all went our separate ways. "If I can get Nadine White to do a book reading at the library, you're all coming, right?"

"Can I tell her that her book is no good?" Dottie took out a cigarette, sticking it in the corner of her mouth and letting it bounce as she talked. "She needs to be told that she needs more substance than a romantic fling and all that hoping to find love again."

"Dottie, I promise. You are going to love her. She's amazing." Abby's smile was brighter than the North Star on the night Jesus was birthed. Well, at least brighter than how I pictured it. "I have to go! I've got to get to some internet and take down that tweet about her being here."

The rest of us stood there watching Abby bolt out the door into the falling snow, leaving her coat on the back of her chair.

"Poor girl." Queenie tsked, clasped her hands, and bended forward to the ground. "I guess I better get to the church. I've got a Jazzercise class to teach and that undercroft gets really cold if they haven't put the heat on."

Queenie gave hugs all around.

"We've got the heat on." Betts moved the chairs from the

circle back to where they belonged. "I made sure Lester knew." Lester was Betts's husband and preacher of the Normal Baptist Church.

"The three of you aren't getting no younger, so you better come join me for some good cardio exercise." Queenie wiggled her fingers into jazz hands before she slipped her hot pink gloves over them.

"Here." Betts had run over to the coffee bar and made to-go cups of coffee. "Take a cup with you. It's cold out there."

Betts was a woman who wore many hats. She not only did everything she could to be a wonderful wife and mother, she ran The Laundry Club, which was doing great, cleaned houses on the side, and was involved with various clubs around town.

Dottie and I said our goodbyes to Betts and put our coats on.

"I sure hope Abby doesn't get her hopes up." Dottie stood on the sidewalk and lit her cigarette.

"I'm worried about that too. She's built her up in her mind to be this wonderful woman. I just hope Nadine White doesn't disappoint her number one fan." I wrapped my hand around the crook of Dottie's arm. "Let's walk on over to the thrift shop and see what decorations Buck's got over there for Nadine's camper."

CHRISTMAS, CRIMINALS, AND CAMPERS is now available to purchase or get in Kindle Unlimited.

RECIPES AND CLEANING HACKS FROM MAE WEST
AND WOMEN OF
NORMAL, KENTUCKY and THE HAPPY TRAILS
CAMPGROUND

HACK #1

RV HACK #1

LAUNDRY DAY WHEN THERE ISN'T A PLACE LIKE THE LAUNDRY CLUB

Nobody likes going to the laundromat, unless it has all the fun things that The Laundry Club has, so unless you have a large, fancy pants RV/camper with a washer and dryer, you will want to try this hack while camping. Just take a bucket and a plunger and use them to wash your clothes. Then you can line dry them in the sun. The bucket and plunger make a great little washing machine, and there is nothing like the smell of clothes line dried in the forest.

CAMPFIRE BREAKFAST SCRAMBLE

INGREDIENTS
- 4 large potatoes
- 1 onion
- 1 dozen eggs
- 2 cups sharp cheddar cheese
- salt & pepper
- ½ cup oil
- 1 pound ground sausage or bacon

INSTRUCTIONS

1. Fry potatoes in oil until soft, then add onion.
2. Move potatoes and onion to the side of the pan, where heat is lower.
3. Scramble and fry sausage.
4. Crack eggs over mixture; scramble until done.
5. Sprinkle with cheese.

GRAB A BAG OF DORITOS

You will never look at Doritos the same after you hear this brilliant hack. Starting a campfire doesn't come naturally to everybody, even your most expert RV'er. After you've created a tent with your campfire wood, put a handful of Doritos in the middle of the tent. Use your matches to light the Doritos on fire and watch one of your favorite snacks turn into the best kindling you've ever seen.

SHRIMP FOIL PACK SUPPER

Foil packs are a must when camping. They are easy to make ahead of time and then pop on the grill with little clean up.

INGREDIENTS

1 lb medium shrimp, peeled and deveined
   3 ears corn, quartered
   1 zucchini, cut into half moons
   2 cloves garlic, minced
   2 tsp ground cumin
   1 tsp crushed red pepper flakes
   Extra-virgin olive oil, for drizzling
   Kosher salt
   Freshly ground black pepper
   2 limes, sliced into rounds
   2 tbsp butter

DIRECTIONS

1. In a large bowl, combine shrimp, corn, zucchini, garlic, cumin, and red pepper flakes. Drizzle with olive oil, season with salt and pepper, and toss until combined.
2. Lay out four rectangles of foil. Divide the shrimp mixture equally between the pieces of foil and top each with a pat of butter and lime slices. Seal the foil packs.
3. Heat grill to high. Add shrimp packs and grill until shrimp is pink, about 10 minutes.
4. Chow down!

SAGE IS THE PERFECT BUG REPELLANT

Mosquitos are never welcome when camping or RVing. They can literally suck the fun out of any trip. Head on over to your local homeopathic shop and grab a bundle of sage. When you're ready to light your campfire and to enjoy your night without those pesky bloodsuckers, throw the sage bundle into the flames. Not only will the sage keep the mosquitos away, it will put off a wonderful smell.

CHOCOLATE BANANA BOATS IN FOIL

INGREDIENTS

1 banana, peeled

2 tbsp miniature marshmallows

2 tbsp semi-sweet chocolate chips

2 tbsp Cinnamon Toast Crunch™ cereal, slightly crushed

Aluminum Foil

INSTRUCTIONS

1. Preheat grill to medium high heat.
2. Slice banana lengthwise and open it slightly. Place on a rectangle of aluminum foil.
3. Sprinkle marshmallows and chocolate chips into the sliced banana.
4. Wrap banana in foil and cook on the grill for 5 to 6 minutes.
5. Unwrap banana and top with cereal.
6. Once it has cooled a little, enjoy with a spoon!

Also By Tonya Kappes

SUNSETS, SABBATICAL, & SCANDAL
TENTS, TRAILS, & TURMOIL
KICKBACKS, KAYAKS, & KIDNAPPING
GEAR, GRILLS, & GUNS
EGGNOG, EXTORTION, & EVERGREENS
ROPES, RIDDLES, & ROBBERIES
PADDLERS, PROMISES, & POISON

Killer Coffee Mystery Series
SCENE OF THE GRIND
MOCAH AND MURDER
FRESHLY GROUND MURDER
COLD BLOODED BREW
DECAFFEINATED SCANDAL
A KILLER LATTE
HOLIDAY ROAST MORTEM
DEAD TO THE LAST DROP
A CHARMING BLEND NOVELLA (CROSSOVER WITH
MAGICAL CURES MYSTERY)
FROTHY FOUL PLAY

Mail Carrier Cozy Mystery
STAMPED OUT
ADDRESS FOR MURDER
ALL SHE WROTE
RETURN TO SENDER
FIRST CLASS KILLER
POST MORTEM

A Ghostly Southern Mystery Series
A GHOSTLY UNDERTAKING
A GHOSTLY GRAVE
A GHOSTLY DEMISE

A GHOSTLY MURDER
A GHOSTLY REUNION
A GHOSTLY MORTALITY
A GHOSTLY SECRET
A GHOSTLY SUSPECT

A Southern Cake Baker Series
(WRITTEN UNDER MAYEE BELL)
CAKE AND PUNISHMENT
BATTER OFF DEAD

Kenni Lowry Mystery Series
FIXIN' TO DIE
SOUTHERN FRIED
AX TO GRIND
SIX FEET UNDER
DEAD AS A DOORNAIL
TANGLED UP IN TINSEL
DIGGIN' UP DIRT

Spies and Spells Mystery Series
SPIES AND SPELLS
BETTING OFF DEAD
GET WITCH or DIE TRYING

A Laurel London Mystery Series
CHECKERED CRIME
CHECKERED PAST
CHECKERED THIEF

A Divorced Diva Beading Mystery Series
A BEAD OF DOUBT SHORT STORY
STRUNG OUT TO DIE

CRIMPED TO DEATH

Olivia Davis Paranormal Mystery Series
SPLITSVILLE.COM
COLOR ME LOVE (novella)
COLOR ME A CRIME

About Tonya

Tonya has written over 65 novels, all of which have graced numerous bestseller lists, including the USA Today. *Best known for stories charged with emotion and humor and filled with flawed characters, her novels have garnered reader praise and glowing critical reviews. She lives with her husband and a very spoiled rescue cat named Ro. Tonya grew up in the small southern Kentucky town of Nicholasville. Now that her four boys are grown men, Tonya writes full-time.*

Learn more about her books here. Find her on Facebook, Twitter, BookBub, and her website.

Sign up to receive her newsletter, where you'll get free books, exclusive bonus content, and news of her releases and sales.

If you liked this book, please take a few minutes to leave a review now! Authors (Tonya included) really appreciate this, and it helps draw more readers to books they might like. Thanks!

Made in the USA
Coppell, TX
25 April 2021